MIRROR, MIRROR

A Collection of Halloween Shorts

Kate Baray

Steve Statham

M. G. Herron

D. F. Jones

S. R. Bond

Copyright

To all the dreamers who see reflections, and wonder.

CONTENTS

THE COVERED MIRROR

KATE BARAY

Fiona brushed a few stray hairs away from her face, careful to use the side of her hand. Her hands were covered in filth—dust mixed with cobwebs and who knew what else. She should have worn gloves. But who would have thought her painfully tidy Aunt Letty would let any part of her home, even her attic, fall into such a state? Maybe she'd been struggling with poor health and Fiona simply hadn't realized? A familiar tightness blossomed in her chest.

Fiona focused all of her attention on her task. On this moment. The past was then, and she was concerned with now. The tight knot loosened.

She shifted her weight back onto her heels. Her knees ached from kneeling, so it was probably time to give up on the chest she'd been digging through and move on to the last corner. She made a face at the stack of dusty boxes waiting for her. As she stood up, her gaze was drawn to a large picture frame draped with an old sheet resting behind the stacked boxes. She hadn't noticed it before.

As she passed by the opening to the attic, she called down the steps, "Just a few more minutes."

Her roommate Libby hollered, "Hurry it up." Her voice got closer, and eventually her head poked up through the attic opening. "I still need to put the final touches on my costume for the Halloween party tonight." She scrunched up her nose. "And it'll take me forever to remove all this grime and touch up my manicure. I am not going to a party with chipped nails."

"Ten minutes," Fiona said. When Libby sighed and nodded, Fiona couldn't hide her grin. "You really are the best. How about I treat you to a quick touch-up at your favorite nail place?"

"Oh, well, that's all right. What's left?"

Fiona pointed to the dark corner with the covered painting.

Libby crawled the rest of the way into the attic. She brushed her hands down the thighs of her yoga pants, leaving dusty prints. "Speaking of Halloween and parties: didn't you tell me your aunt had a thing for Halloween?"

"Yeah." But Fiona's response was automatic. She was too busy untangling the sheet that had caught on the ornate frame to pay much attention to Libby. Once freed, the object underneath revealed itself to be a mirror, not a painting after all. "Oh, pretty." She lifted it up to show Libby.

"Nice. Not your usual style—a little fanciful—but you should definitely keep that one. Ohmygod." Libby started to bounce on her toes. "It's perfect! We have to bring it to the party."

The loops and curvy decorations framing the oval mirror were metal of some sort, making it heavy, and Fiona's arms were beginning to ache. She set it down quickly. "Yeah. I forgot about that."

The party was being thrown by their close friend Becky. Fiona and Libby, as well as a few other women, had agreed to bring by a few decorations before the party. "Something Halloween-ish" had been the request.

"Yeah, I forgot, too. But with something like this, Becky will never know we waited until the last minute. Which is what makes it perfect." Libby raised her eyebrows. "Right?"

"Agreed. But we should probably clean it up a little." Fiona leaned down to inspect the metal frame. Rubbing hard at the edge with the pad of her thumb, she said, "I think it might be silver."

"Oh. Maybe we shouldn't, then?"

"No. It's fine." Fiona shook out the old sheet a bit then wrapped it around the mirror. "If you head down first, I can hand it down."

Libby headed down the narrow attic ladder. "This is going to be such a great party. Wicked costumes, fluorescent drinks, masks, glitter—God, I love Halloween." When she got to the bottom, she looked up and said, "Aunt Letty would be glad to see you getting out."

Fiona pushed the familiar tightness away and grabbed the mirror. Turning to hand the mirror down, she pasted on a fake smile and said, "Yeah."

***

Half an hour later, Fiona and Libby sat cross-legged on the kitchen floor, the antique mirror between them.

"We've been polishing like mad for ten minutes, and we've barely made a dent." Libby arched her back. "This is actually hard work. I think my arms might be sore tomorrow."

"Yeah. I'm starting to think that the tarnish might add a little creepy, Halloween-ish charm. It wasn't like

Aunt Letty to let something valuable go uncared for. It's probably silver plate."

"Right. Silver plate, sterling." Libby lifted the stained cloth in her hand. "Both require silver polish. Not cool."

"I'm gonna work on it for a few more minutes, but why don't you head out and get your nails done before it's too late? Cash is in the coffee can on top of the fridge."

Libby dropped her polish-stained rag and jumped to her feet. "Thank you," she said with her eyes raised upward, and then she did a little happy dance.

Trying not to laugh, Fiona said, "It's not that bad. You get more of a workout with free weights at the gym."

Libby gave her a serious look. "Not the same thing."

Fiona bit her lip, refraining from commenting that at least polishing silver was free. She bent back down to her polishing. As she made gentle, repetitive circular motions, her mind eventually drifted to her aunt's funeral. No. She wouldn't—couldn't—do that. She lived in the now. In this moment.

"Good enough," Fiona announced to the empty room as she stood up. Glancing at the kitchen clock, she was surprised to see a half hour had passed. Well, not so surprising, given the ache in both her arms. "At least the grime is gone."

She was suddenly tempted to hang it on the wall. Silly, because it was going with them to the party, but Fiona indulged the urge. She took down a print from the living room wall, and as she examined the mirror's hanging mechanism—a simple wire string across the back—she noticed a faded ink scribble on the back.

She flipped on the overhead light. The paper backing of the mirror was brittle and there were a few small tears, but the scribblings had been spared from damage. She studied the inked lines and finally deciphered what looked like a name: Kovar. Maybe George. George Kovar?

Fiona pulled up the web browser on her phone and googled George Kovar, expecting to find some Yellow Pages hits, a few social media links, and a guy or two selling used cars or original art. The odds and ends of different people's lives that appear when you randomly google a name. But several of the hits linked to a Georg Kovar, early twentieth-century psychiatrist and philanthropist.

"Huh. A philanthropist sounds like a good candidate to own a silver-framed mirror, doesn't he?" Fiona clicked on one of the links, but a loud meow made her jump. "Ralph!"

Her cat Ralph, quietly lounging on the sofa while she'd been puttering with her new mirror, had let loose a strident demand for attention.

"You're right, Ralph. I am not talking to myself. I'm absolutely talking to you." Fiona scratched Ralph's jaw and petted him until he'd had enough and hopped off the sofa.

Fiona pocketed her phone and went back to the mirror. But after studying it for several minutes, she couldn't make out the message above the name. All she could pick out were a few common words: *the, your, a, and*. And something that looked like *uncover*. She should probably have an expert look at it. If the mirror really had belonged to this do-gooder Kovar guy, then it might be valuable. But again, that just didn't agree with what Fiona knew of Aunt Letty. And she knew her aunt very, very well. Fiona shoved her hair out of her face and picked up the mirror. Time to hang the thing. That had been the plan.

After a little trial and error, she got the wire behind the mirror to catch on both nails. *Voila*—her mirror was hung.

Fiona stepped back with some satisfaction and inspected the ornate mirror. The reflection had a distorted quality, and the tarnish that stubbornly clung made the frame quite dark. But she liked it. As she turned to go, movement just on the edge of her vision made her whip back to the mirror.

Fiona couldn't help but laugh at herself. Of course there was movement. She'd been turning, which meant that her image in the mirror had been, too.

But as she turned her back on the mirror, the hairs on the back of her neck rose.

***

Cobweb- and tarnish-free, dressed in a cute black dress, and hair almost dry, Fiona was on her way—just barely—to becoming "sexy witch." Apparently, that was her costume for the night. She headed to the kitchen, where she knew a pre-party drink would be waiting.

Fiona walked into the kitchen just as Libby was pouring two long shots from a shaker. "I'm not sure why I left my costume up to you."

Libby looked up from her bartending duties. "Because I'm fabulous with costumes, and you're a big dud." She held out a glass to Fiona. "And you trust me implicitly."

"Yes to that first part, and emphatically *no* to the trust thing. Lemon drop?"

Libby nodded. "Cheers." She tapped glasses with Fiona then downed her shot.

Fiona sipped hers. "I know the problem. I'm lazy, and you make me go to parties that require planning."

Libby tipped her head to the side. She seemed to be considering her words carefully. "You need to get out a little. Especially now." She looked like she wanted to say more, but changed her mind.

"You had some kind of special makeup planned for sexy witch?"

Libby brightened immediately. "I've got some great black liquid eyeliner for you. And some striped thigh-high stockings, a cape, and I found this fabulous hat." Her voice faded as she headed to the back bathroom. "Come on already."

Thirty minutes later, Fiona blinked slowly at her image in the mirror. She was all eyelashes and liner and glittery shadow. Like a witch had met a '70s glam rocker, and she was their very confused love child. It was beyond cool. "My eyelashes weigh about a pound each. I feel like I'm blinking in slow motion."

Libby waved her comment away. "It's the fake eyelashes, but that goes away in a few minutes. You won't even notice them by the time we leave. Speaking of, get your butt in gear. We need to leave pretty soon so we can arrive early and deliver our Halloween deco contribution."

"Right—and thanks." Fiona headed to her bedroom, but she couldn't resist a quick look in the newly hung mirror. She did a double take.

A faint outline appeared next to her reflection. Heart in her throat, pulse leaping, Fiona stood frozen as the image sharpened. A second, smaller image of her.

Fiona stumbled back, away from the mirror. Her mirror image and the smaller image did the same. She opened her mouth, but nothing came out. She tried to call, to scream, but couldn't. Why couldn't she scream? Panic gripped her, made her vision swim, her breath shorten.

Breathe. Just breathe. Breathe. She thought it over and over until she was actually doing it. And when her vision cleared, all she saw was a pale, glamorous, gasping version of herself in the mirror. Just the one. No double image. No smaller twin lurking to the side.

Libby walked up behind her decked out as a fairy creature. "You hung the mirror—cool. The glam style looks even better in this mirror. It's a little like candlelight, isn't it? Softens everything around the edges." She must have finally noticed Fiona's pallor, because she frowned and turned from Fiona's mirror image to Fiona herself. "Are you okay?"

Fiona swallowed and shook her head. "Yeah, sorry. I'm fine. Uh, do you mind grabbing the mirror and wrapping it up?"

"Sure. Did you already order our ride?"

"Just about to. Be right back. I need to grab my hat and cape." Fiona tried to smile, but couldn't quite manage it. And again, as soon as she turned her back on the mirror, the hairs on the back of her neck lifted.

When Fiona walked into her room, she was distracted by the piece of art sitting on her bed: a beautifully embellished—but enormous—black witch's hat. "Libby—I can't wear this hat," Fiona called down the hall. "It's massive."

"The hat absolutely makes the outfit. You have to wear the hat."

Fiona wasn't convinced, but after she'd ordered their ride, she tried on both it and the cape. Slowly, she looked in her dresser mirror. And her completely normal, single reflection stared back. She gave her head a tiny shake, then grabbed her phone, keys, and wallet and stuffed them all into a small black evening bag that she slung over her shoulder.

When Fiona stepped out in the hall, Libby quickly said, "You have to *arrive* in the hat. If it drives you batty, we'll stash it in a spare bedroom."

"That's fine. It *is* gorgeous." Fiona's gaze fell to the bundled-up mirror under Libby's arm. "Maybe it's not a good idea to bring it."

Libby gave her a probing look. "Are you sure you're okay? You've been acting a little oddly this evening."

"Yeah. Of course. I'm fine." Fiona adjusted the collar of her cape. "Let's wait outside. Our driver should be here any minute."

"Really, Fiona. If you want to stay in, maybe talk about your aunt—"

"No!" Fiona took a breath. "Sorry. No, I'm fine. Let's just go. And of course we're bringing the mirror."

***

It wasn't a very long ride, only about ten minutes, to Becky's house. Which was fortunate, because the tension on the ride over had made Fiona edgy. Whether it was riding in close quarters with that damn mirror, or trying to avoid Libby's questioning eyes, or even the frantic avoidance of her own thoughts on the events of the evening—Fiona wasn't sure. Whatever the cause, she couldn't get out of the car fast enough when they arrived at Becky's.

Libby joined her at the door just as Becky opened it. So Libby could only glare covertly and grunt quietly as she shifted the heavy frame under her arm.

"I'm guessing that's your Halloween decoration?" Becky pointed at the bundle then ushered them in. There was only one other early decorator inside who'd beat them.

"It is." Libby set it down on the floor in front of the sofa and started to unwrap it. "There is a small chance it's actually worth some money, so we should probably be a little careful." She chewed on her lip then added quickly, "And it belonged to Fiona's aunt."

A short silence followed as Becky and Ashley, the other early arrival, glanced uncomfortably in Fiona's direction.

"I'm fine. I'm absolutely, completely fine. People get old. They die. It happens and we move on." Fiona could feel the heat in her face and the erratic thump of the rapid pulse in her throat. Why couldn't they all just leave it the fuck alone? The muscles in her abdomen started to cramp. She *was* fine, dammit. Everything was fine. She was fine. *Just breathe.* When the tight feeling had faded, she asked, "Any chance of a drink?"

A dazed Becky led Fiona to the drinks table on the back patio. Becky had cleverly premixed a few punches that were available in glass urns: one bright orange, another deep purple, and a third a sparkling turquoise.

"These are beautiful, Becky. I'm sorry I'm such a grump. I've just had a really weird day. Which should I try?"

Becky gave her a smile full of sympathy—too much sympathy. "I like the bright blue one." When Fiona nodded, she poured two drinks. "I think grape for Libby."

When they got back with the drinks, there were a few more arrivals and they were all clustered around the mirror.

"You won't believe." Libby took her drink and swallowed a mouthful. "Dave thinks your mirror might be a big deal. Well, a sort of big deal. Tell her, Dave."

A medium-height guy with thinning blond hair nodded. "I'd guess it's at least a hundred years old, based on the quality of the mirror surface—but I'm definitely not an expert. You need to have a pro take a look. But what's really cool is this message on the back. I can just make out the name. That means with a little research you might be able to trace ownership back a few generations. Pieces with a story almost always get more money." He blushed. "Sorry, it's pretty cool, though."

"Yeah. That's really interesting." Fiona gave him an encouraging smile.

All the while Dave was speaking, Fiona had avoided looking into the mirror. As casually as she could, she scanned the faces of the people gathered, some friends and some strangers. No one looked the least concerned. She wanted to thump herself. Maybe she'd seen a few too many horror films lately. Or she'd been working too hard. She knew she hadn't been getting the best sleep lately. Whatever was going on, she wasn't crazy. And she definitely wasn't actually seeing some demon manifestation in her aunt's old mirror.

She turned to look at the mirror.

The second—her mind stuttered as it searched for a label—*her*, but not her. A reflection, but autonomous. It was a thing. That thing in the mirror, it was no longer a mirror image. It showed up crisply on the distorted glass.

It looked sad. Its eyes were huge in a pale copy of Fiona's face, the corners of her lips pulled down. Looking at that woman—at that perversion of herself—made Fiona want to cry. Desperately.

She closed her eyes, unable to look without breaking into sobs.

Libby's voice reached her, though it sounded far away. "Fiona. Fiona."

Someone shook her arm slightly. She angled her body away from the mirror before she opened her eyes. "Sorry."

"Are you okay? You went all pale. You definitely look witchy now." Libby's eyes were wide. She reached over and pried Fiona's fingers away from her drink. "And maybe no more Blue Skies for you. We both know Becky's concoctions have a big kick."

Fiona giggled. She felt lightheaded. Like her feet weren't quite touching the ground. "Yeah. Remember that time, on the roof, when you—"

"Okay. That's enough of that. You promised not to tell that story. Ever."

Fiona blinked. She could feel her feet again. And the aching fingers that had frantically clutched at her drink glass. "Right."

Fiona hadn't noticed, but Libby had been leading her gently away from the small crowd and the mirror.

And then Fiona heard the murmurs. She only caught a few words, but that was more than enough. "Died suddenly. Very close. Not coping." *Screw them.* Kind words. Words filled with sympathy. *Screw all of them.* The tight ball that seemed to live in Fiona's chest expanded, making her breath catch.

"Hey." Libby rubbed her back. "It's okay."

Fiona stood up taller and stepped away from Libby. "I'm fine. Really." She even managed what must have been a passable smile, because Libby relaxed.

"You're sure?"

"Yeah. One stout drink and no dinner, and here I am. You know what a lightweight I am. I'll just find the appetizers. A little food and I'll be good to go."

More people had filtered in, and the music started. Libby looked around at the crowd then back to Fiona. "You're sure?"

"Yes. Go. Have fun and party like the wild woman I know you are." Fiona gave her best friend a gentle nudge toward a particularly attractive pirate.

Libby eyed the pirate, then Fiona, then the pirate again. "Well, all right. But I'm watching you, girl."

Fiona smiled at Libby's retreating fairy wings. But her smile quickly faded. What the hell was going on with that mirror? And Fiona was pretty damn sure it was the mirror and not her. If she were losing her mind, wouldn't she be seeing weird, almost-her images all over the place? And why an image of herself—altered though the image might be?

She sighed. Who was she kidding? She had no idea what crazy looked like. For all she knew, this was it. She reached her hands up to rub her face then stopped, remembering the sexy witch eye makeup. She was all about living in the now these days, so that's what she was going to do. And her stomach was definitely grumbling. She went in search of the appetizer table.

**

Overall, a good night. She'd flirted with a passable Thor, managed to avoid the persistent, antique-loving

Dave and any further conversation he might attempt about that vile mirror, and—best of all—the mirror had disappeared into some distant corner where Fiona had yet to spot it again.

Fiona set her empty glass down and excused herself from the small group she'd been chatting with. She looked around for her hostess and spotted her next to the drinks table.

"Becky, remind me where the bathroom is."

Becky pointed to the hallway. "Second door on the left. Oh, I forgot—"

Fiona missed the last part because nature was urgently calling after two club sodas and another Blue Sky. And she just knew there'd be a wait.

When there was no line, Fiona wanted to do a little jig—but she'd wait until she was finished, thank you very much.

Business attended to and feeling much better, Fiona moved to the sink to wash her hands—and there it was: her mirror. Before she looked away, she caught a vague impression of fake cobwebs, plastic spiders, and black and orange tinsel.

Her back to the mirror, Fiona tried to convince herself that the cheery Halloween party vibe Becky had created in the bathroom was *all* that was in the room with her. That no bizarre devils lurked in the mirror. But the raised hairs on the back of her neck said otherwise.

Later she'd wonder why she hadn't just left. Walked out of the bathroom, left the party, given the damn mirror to Becky so she could be haunted by whatever the hell was inside it. But in that moment, Fiona couldn't leave.

Fiona convinced herself the pricking at the back of her neck was her imagination or an overly efficient air-conditioning system. All she had to do was turn around, and she'd see there was nothing there. Easy.

A sick feeling in her gut, she turned and looked into the mirror.

It screamed at Fiona. Pounded its fists against the mirror. Pounded its fists again and again. So hard. Fiona stood frozen in horror. Not moving, not breathing. Surely the mirror would shatter into a thousand pieces. But the thing pounded even harder, flinging its whole body against the mirror. Violent anger contorted its features. The vitriol of the thing was terrifying, grotesque. And Fiona could only stare—transfixed by the thing with her face.

No. She shook her head. *No.* That wasn't her. She stumbled backward, shaking her head. Not her. Someone else. In a low, harsh voice Fiona barely recognized as her own, she said, "You are not me."

The creature mouthed one word: yes.

Fiona backed away. Her heel snagged. She flailed, snatched at the air, grabbed a handful of shower curtain. Almost steady, she started to move—and the curtain crashed to the floor. A small, frightened whine escaped her lips, and she fell to the ground.

Knocking. Louder knocking. "Hello? Are you all right in there?"

Fiona's jaw throbbed. She'd probably just passed out in the bathroom. No. Not okay. She licked her lips, cleared her throat. "I'm fine." Her voice came out a tiny squeak. She cleared her throat again. "I'm fine," she called, much more loudly this time. "Give me just a minute."

She would not look at the mirror. Not looking at the mirror. Easy enough once she realized she was sprawled in the tub. Shit. She steeled herself for pain she knew would come when she heaved herself out. One, two—oh, God. That hurt. Her ankle was twisted. Her jaw ached like a sonofabitch. And she'd clearly banged her left elbow. But she was at least on the bathroom floor now and not passed out in the tub.

She grabbed the doorknob and hauled herself to her knees. Unlocking and cracking the door, she peeked out into the hall. Whew. Just two people. Of course, one of them was Dave.

From Fiona's position on her knees, she gave him a friendly little wave and a weak smile.

The woman who'd knocked on the door moved out of the way so he could approach.

"Um, I had a little slip and fall in the bathroom. Do you mind fetching Libby?" Fiona tried for an apologetic but not pathetic tone. But there was no way to get around it. She knew she was pathetic. Her makeup had to be smeared to hell, she was still on her knees, and, given how clammy she felt, she had to be white as a sheet.

"No problem. I'll be right back." As Dave left, he spoke to the other woman. "Uh, can you, you know…"

"Of course." The blond woman turned to Fiona, leaned down, and said, "If you back up a little, I can open the door. Is that okay?"

Fiona rested her head on the doorjamb. "This is so incredibly embarrassing." But she inched back. As she did, the woman carefully pushed until the door could open all the way.

"I'm Kenna. Happy to assist in times of great embarrassment and mild injury—especially if you're willing to do the same."

Fiona laughed. "Fiona. And thank you, Kenna. It's very nice to meet you."

Kenna was leaning down to help Fiona, when the strangest thing happened. She paused and gave the mirror a close, narrow-eyed look. Before Fiona could comment or ask if she saw anything unusual, the moment had passed. Kenna gave her steadying hand, and Fiona did her damnedest to hobble out of that bathroom as fast as she could.

When she and Kenna had made it halfway down the hall, they stopped.

"Can I prop you up against the wall for a second? I'm in desperate need of a pee. Apparently being pregnant means you pee every two seconds—and it's been a little longer than that by now." Kenna grinned.

"Sorry, I didn't even realize…"

Kenna's smile widened. She really was a very pretty woman. "I accept the compliment. I'm five and half months." She leaned in to kiss Fiona's cheek. Quietly, she said, "Everything will be fine."

And then she was gone, disappeared into the bathroom—with the mirror.

"Oh, Lord. What have you done?" Libby called when she saw Fiona.

Fiona shook her head. "Just slipped and fell in the bathroom. I'm pretty sure no major damage was done. But I would love to get home. It's been a really long day."

Libby touched Fiona's jaw.

"Ow! Watch it."

"Yeah. I'm coming home with you. Let me just call a ride." Libby whipped out her phone and had arranged an Uber ride in less than thirty seconds. She could be frighteningly efficient in emergencies. "Let me just grab your Aunt Letty's mirror."

"No!" When Fiona realized how bizarre her rabid response must seem, she said, "I mean, let's leave it for now. I can pick it up later."

Libby gave her an odd look, but agreed.

***

The last thing Fiona remembered before falling asleep was that her comforter had never felt so soft and that this was the safest she'd felt since finding the mirror.

The feeling of safety and comfort didn't last through the night. Fiona's dreams had been troubled by images of her doppelganger appearing in every mirror she passed. Her dream house had been filled with covered mirrors. Sheets were draped over every reflective surface in her home. When she woke, Fiona had a strong feeling that the antique mirror had been swathed, placed in the corner of Aunt Letty's attic, and left unpolished over the years for a very good reason. The thing wasn't safe.

She glanced at the clock. Eleven thirty. She'd slept well past her usual time. No wonder she'd had such unsettling dreams. Ugh. She couldn't leave that damn mirror at Becky's house. She needed to get the thing back and pack it up again. She grabbed her second pillow and pulled it over her face. Or she could just stay here in bed forever.

A light knock on her door caught her attention.

"Hey, Libby. I'm awake." Fiona's voice came out muffled because she hadn't moved the pillow.

Libby cracked the door. "I thought I'd head out and grab some Thai takeaway for lunch. Want me to pick up anything for you?"

"Yes, please. My usual." Fiona still refused to come out from under her pillow. "Thank you."

The door clicked shut.

Fiona wallowed in indecision for a few more minutes, then an amazing thought occurred to her. It wasn't Halloween. Today was not Halloween. Maybe her cursed mirror only worked on Halloween. Could it be so simple? Maybe?

The hope was enough to get her out of bed. But on the off chance there was no correlation, and the haunting, possession—whatever—was year round, she'd still have Becky wrap it.

Surprisingly, she found her ankle only mildly tender, and her elbow seemed completely fine. But then she cracked a wide yawn and tears immediately gathered in her eyes. Tenderly, she touched her jaw. "Ow. Ugh. Serves me right, freaking out in a confined space with lots of hard surfaces."

Bleary-eyed, she made her way to the kitchen. She just needed a cup of coffee. Then she saw the mirror, hanging on the wall where she'd hung it yesterday. Much as she tried to look away, she couldn't.

The moment her eyes met the mirror, that screaming, violent, angry perversion of herself stepped out of the mirror. Fiona tried to scream—but her mouth opened and no sound emerged. Terror chilled her—froze her. The tiny hairs on her body stood at attention.

It stepped close. She tried—failed—to back away. Locked joints. Stiff muscles. It was so close. Its cold breath chilled her wet cheek. Anger. Disappointment. And then—it touched her. Was inside her. Clawed her. Clawed at that tight spot. That small, clenched ball in her chest. Fiona's head swam. Surely she was dying.

She was disoriented; the world tilted the wrong way. Cold tile pressed against her hip, her cheek. As Fiona tried to remember how, when, she'd fallen to the ground... Suddenly she felt it. A hole filled. An empty space occupied. And the terror returned—heart hammering, pulse thudding, loud rushing in her ears. She was possessed. She was dying. She was consumed. Tears ran down her face. And the tears became hiccupping sobs. And the sobs turned to choked gasps. And she cried and cried.

Grief had found her. It filled her up. Filled the hollow space inside, the one that felt like constant, tight, clenched hurt. That ball of nothing that grew when Aunt Letty had slipped away. Gone from life without a goodbye. Buried in the ground with no real farewell. Abandoning Fiona without any warning. Tearing a hole inside her very being.

She'd never grieved—couldn't let herself feel the pain. Terrified she'd be overwhelmed. But the grief, the sorrow, the anger, the blackness of loss had found her. And now it consumed her. Fiona's body racked with sobs as she finally recognized that perverted thing in the mirror. Her. It was her. Emotions she'd denied. Feelings she'd pushed away.

But wrapped up tightly with that grief was the incredible love, the affection of a lifetime. All the good she'd felt for her favorite person in the world. Sometimes her best friend. Sometimes her mentor. Sometimes her confidante. Her wonderful Aunt Letty. Gone forever. Never, ever coming back.

Fiona curled into a tiny ball on the tile and cried. Cried for her aunt, who'd died too early and all alone. Cried for herself, for losing someone so dear. Cried because she wasn't sure she could handle the overwhelming sadness that wanted to swallow her whole. Cried because she didn't know what else to do.

***

Libby found Fiona curled up on the floor in the living room. From her perspective on the floor, Fiona could see their Thai takeout drop to the tile and Libby's feet rushing toward her.

"Fiona."

Libby didn't ask if she was all right. Didn't tell her she'd be fine. She just sat down next to her on the tile floor. Finally, a long time later, Libby hugged her and got up. She came back with a damp washcloth.

Fiona wasn't sure what to say, so she told her the truth. "I miss Aunt Letty."

Libby handed her the washcloth. "I know."

Fiona took the cloth then rolled on her back and covered her face with it. Her eyes felt sticky and gritty at the same time. She could only imagine the gooey mess her tears had made mingling with the eye makeup she'd forgotten to remove last night. "At least tell me the fake eyelashes got lost somewhere along the way."

Libby let out a tiny giggle. "We'll go with that."

"Ugh. I feel like shit."

Her tone serious again, Libby said, "I know."

She didn't tell Fiona she'd been a little bit crazy the last few weeks. She didn't accuse her of not caring. Of not dealing with her grief. Of losing her mind. Of being a bitch. Because Libby understood. Fiona had loved her aunt so very much. And the hurt had just been too much.

"Can I get you a cup of coffee or something?" Libby asked as she stood up.

Before Fiona could reply, the doorbell rang.

"You're not expecting anyone?" Libby asked as she headed to the door.

Peeking over the top of the washcloth, Fiona said, "No. Definitely not." She sat up and wiped her eyes as best she could then flipped the cloth over and wiped her face. She must look frightening. Sexy witch turned evil witch, probably.

"Fiona. There's a woman here about your aunt's mirror."

"Ask her in." When Libby gave her a strange look, Fiona nodded emphatically. "Really. Please."

Carefully, Fiona stood up. She dropped the washcloth on a side table and approached the woman who might just make her day. "I'm Fiona. Sorry." She gestured vaguely at her PJs. "Rough night. How can I help you?"

"I'm Gwen. I'm here to inquire about an antique mirror. Silver, with an inscription on the back? My daughter thought you might consider selling it."

The blond pregnant woman. It had to have been. She was the only other person to look at the mirror like it was something…weird. "I don't suppose your daughter is a pretty blond, several months pregnant?"

"That's her." Gwen smiled, her eyes crinkling happily at the corners. "She happened to hear a young man at the party mention the inscription on the back. I'm interested in antiques and have family friends with a close connection to the Kovars, so it seemed like a wonderful find."

Wonderful find, her ass. And Gwen wasn't exactly what Fiona would have expected an antiques expert to look like. Skinny jeans, a tight T-shirt, black leather jacket, and All-Stars. Fiona tilted her head, trying to wrap her emotionally exhausted brain around the idea of the woman in front of her as an antiques dealer. Maybe more a collector. Definitely something fishy, but Fiona was beyond caring.

Then the actual meaning of Gwen's words finally pierced Fiona's inadequately functioning mind: the mirror gone. Fiona almost choked in her haste to speak. "Sold."

Libby gave Gwen a polite smile. "Um, just a second." She pulled Fiona off to the side. Very quietly, she said, "I don't think you're really in a good place to be making decisions, especially decisions about something potentially valuable, right now. And it was your aunt's."

"She had it locked up in the attic for a very good reason." Fiona tried to look as trustworthy and not crazy as she could manage in her PJs and with her raccoon eyes. "Trust me."

"If you're sure—"

"So completely sure and with no doubts. I have never been more certain. I want that thing gone." Fiona headed back to salvation—a.k.a. Gwen, the not-quite-typical antiques dealer—before Libby could stop her. "I'm very interested in selling it."

"How about fifteen thousand cash?" Gwen dug around in the large bag that hung from her shoulder and produced a thick envelope.

"Wait. We haven't even had it valued. How do we know that's a fair price?" Libby looked back and forth between Gwen and Fiona like they'd both lost their minds.

"It's fine. Fifteen is great. It's yours." Fiona took the envelope before Gwen could change her mind. "But do you mind getting it yourself? It's just there on the wall." She pointed over her shoulder without looking at it.

"Of course." Gwen hovered uncertainly next to Fiona for a brief moment, then she quickly said, "You'll be fine. I'm certain of it." Then she whisked the mirror off the wall and was walking out the front door. She paused in the doorway. "I'll keep it safe." Then she was gone.

Fiona stared at the closed door. What exactly had just happened? And who was Gwen? She'd obviously known something was up with the mirror. But what exactly? And how did Gwen know? But the real question was: did Fiona really want to know the answers?

"Lib—let's eat that Thai food, if it's salvageable."

THE END

ON WINGS OF STEEL

STEVE STATHAM

October 28

Jean watched through the blinds as her daughter's Toyota pulled into the driveway.

Mixed feelings welled up inside her.

She always wanted to see Hannah, of course, but...well. There were some things Jean just didn't feel like talking about today, and Hannah had a way of bringing up a subject and not letting it rest.

Jean shook her head at her own pettiness.

The girl has lost her father. She needs you now more than ever.

She made her way from her bedroom window to the living room and sat in the oversized chair, letting it swallow her. Her eyes drifted to the three items in the entryway. The mirror dominated the space, if not the whole house. Rob had bought it for her as a first anniversary present, at a time when they really couldn't afford custom pieces. It had been the first thing they'd hung when they moved into this house, and the mirror settled into the spot as if it had been made for it.

Below the mirror was the bench Rob had constructed from wood salvaged from his grandfather's barn. Underneath the bench were his work boots, exactly where he'd left them on that final day.

Jean heard Hannah's footsteps on the front porch and then cold sunlight invaded the house as she opened the door. Hannah had only recently moved out of the house and hadn't yet gotten into the habit of knocking before entering her childhood home.

"Hi, Mom. Just stopping by to see how you're doing."

"Hi sweetheart," Jean said, rising from the chair and hugging her daughter. "Did you get off work early?"

"I traded some shifts," she said as she entered. Hannah glanced around the living room, as if conducting an inspection. Jean knew she was checking for signs of disorder or sloth, or any other indicators of depression. Jean tried to accept the scrutiny with grace. Her own friends had been watching her closely too. Everyone was worried. Rob and Jean had been childhood sweethearts. Nobody could imagine one without the other.

"Would you like some tea, dear?"

"Hot tea? Love some," Hannah said, and slumped onto the couch, stretching out. "It hasn't really warmed up yet out there."

Jean busied herself in the kitchen, pulling her kettle from the shelf and searching through the available teas.

"I saw Maggie today," Hannah said. "She asked me to tell you hi."

Jean filled the kettle and placed it on the burner. She tried to remember who Maggie was. Since Rob's passing, the list of well-wishers had grown long, stretching all the way into casual acquaintances she hadn't seen for years.

"Tell her thank you."

Jean poured the tea and then cradled the warm mug in her hands while her daughter chatted about work. Jean watched her daughter closely as she spun her story about last Friday's shift. It was a two-way street, this monitoring of each other since Rob's death. Hannah's speech seemed a bit rushed, forced even, but Jean had figured out that just being together and talking about unrelated subjects helped Hannah cope.

They finished their tea and Hannah carried the cups over to the sink. She glanced up and frowned as something in the entryway caught her eye. Hannah pointed to the bench.

"Are those Dad's old work boots?"

Jean nodded.

"Are you ever going to put them away?"

She sighed. "Someday. But not right now. I'm not ready to pack away all your father's things yet."

"I'm not sure that's real healthy, Mom."

Jean almost smiled at that. Hannah was all of twenty-two, but was already acting as if her mother needed supervision. Jean was only forty-three herself, and sometimes it still amazed her that this adult before her was actually her own child. She and Rob had started young and it was a good thing they had, she reflected now. Their time together was a lot shorter than she'd thought it would be.

"I like them under there. They'll stay."

Hannah nodded, uncertainty coloring her features, but she said no more about it. She returned to the living room and gathered up her sweater.

"I gotta go, Mom. I'm supposed to meet Kim and Erica for happy hour."

Jean stood and walked her to the door. They stepped out on the porch and Jean felt a twinge of surprise at the chill in the air.

When did that cool front roll in? Has it really been a couple days since I went outside?

Hannah stepped off the porch and then turned around, reached out, and squeezed Jean's hand. "Kinda weird not seeing all the Halloween decorations out. Y'all are. . ." She hesitated then, and Jean knew it was the struggle between "y'all" and "you." "You're famous for your Halloween staging. The kids on the block are going to be disappointed. I'll miss it too," she said, her voice trailing off.

"They can survive for a year without me," Jean said. "Maybe next year."

"Are you sure, Mom? I'll be happy to help you put it all up. It might get you back into the normal swing of things..."

"No," she replied. "Halloween was our day, and this first year without him I'm going to keep it for myself."

Hannah held her mother's eye for a long moment and then nodded. "Okay, Mom. Call me if you need anything."

Jean watched her daughter drive off and then returned to the house and the oversized chair. She sat in silence for a while, annoyed at herself for being so short with Hannah. The chair held her in a warm embrace and she curled up into it, suddenly feeling small.

She looked across the room at the boots and wondered if Hannah was right. Then her eyes tracked up to the mirror and sadness hit her in a sudden wave.

Rob had purchased the mirror at one of the local craft fairs, from an eccentric vendor of the type you occasionally saw at those types of events. As Rob had told the story, the man had actually been reluctant to sell his handiwork, but Rob had known he had to have it from the moment first spied the unique object. He was going to buy it for Jean for their first anniversary, and that was all there was to it.

She still remembered unboxing the gift and the thrill that it had sent through her.

The mirror had a wide stainless steel frame, brushed to a rich sheen. But its most striking features were the steel owls that adorned all four sides of the frame. The craftsmanship of the metalwork had astonished her then and still did today. Each of the owls was detailed with cuts and scoring of the metal that imitated the texture of feathers with an uncanny realism.

The four owls were all different. At the top, the owl's wings were spread wide and its talons reached out as if you were the prey about to be plucked from the ground. The bottom owl was a front three-quarter view of the bird in flight, and Jean had never ceased marveling at how the artist had captured that perspective in metal. On the left side, the owl was perched at rest on a tree branch, its eyes closed. On the right, the steel bird looked as it was emerging from the surface of the frame itself. Its eyes were very much open.

More than once Jean had stood in front of the mirror and stared at the owls, wondering how anyone could have breathed so much life into metal.

She closed her eyes and let the afternoon drift past. Her thoughts returned to Rob, as they did several times a day. This time, she went back to the beginning. She could remember their first meeting with a warm intensity that never faded.

They were eight. It was Halloween.

Like any American kid, Jean had always looked forward to Halloween, but that year had vexed her. She hadn't been able to make up her mind between being a pirate or a princess, and so had assembled two costumes so she could decide at the last minute. When the hour for trick-or-treating rolled around, she decided to wear both.

She walked out into the young night wearing a princess gown and tiara, along with an eye patch and a plastic cutlass cinched around her waist. When she joined her friends she saw them all exchange smirking glances, but everyone was too eager to begin collecting candy to say anything rude.

Most of the adults didn't get it. At the first house they stopped at, the woman cheerfully identified all the costumes of Jean's friends, then turned toward her. "And are you...Tinkerbell?"

At the next house the elderly woman only said, "Oh you poor dear! What happened to your eye?"

By the end of the block and two more such encounters, she began to hang toward the back of her circle of friends, ducking in at the last second with her head down and bag extended to collect her candy.

Jean trudged away from the house on the corner, trailing behind her friends, and noticed a boy crossing the street by himself. He walked right up to her and looked her up and down. "You're a pirate princess," he stated matter-of-factly.

A thrill ran through her. Someone understood her costume! *He got it!*

"Uh huh."

"That's cool."

"Thanks."

"I like your bloody sword."

"Thanks."

He was wearing grayish-silver duct tape wrapped around his body and a boxy helmet covered in tinfoil. The cutout for the face was slightly lopsided and he had to tilt his head to look into her eyes.

"What kind of astronaut are you?"

"The real kind. Not like the Star Wars kind," he said, and then frowned. "But everyone keeps asking if I'm a mummy."

She smiled at him. "Nobody understands my costume either."

He smiled back. "I'm Rob."

"I'm Jean."

He pointed down the street. "Have you been to that house? I hear they're giving away big boxes of Sweet Tarts."

"No, I've only been down this side of the street."

"Come with me! I want to go there before they run out."

Jean looked back for her friends but saw they had already headed in the other direction around the block. She turned back to Rob and nodded. They ran to the house. Jean could still clearly remember the exhilaration she felt at the simple freedom of running down the street, just the two of them, at night.

Rob rang the doorbell. After what seemed like an eternity but was surely only seconds, the door swung open.

"I'm a real astronaut and she's a pirate princess," he shouted. "Trick or treat!"

The middle-aged woman at the door raised an eyebrow but grinned and reached into her bowl of candy. She pulled out four large boxes of Sweet Tarts and placed two each in their bags. "Why so you are," she said. "Best costumes I've seen all night."

They ran off laughing but stopped almost immediately and sat on a curb in front of a darkened house. "*Two* boxes," she said, reaching in to grab one. "I've never got two big boxes like that before."

"Me either. What a great street."

They each ripped open the thin cardboard packaging, even though they knew they weren't supposed to until they got home, and popped pieces of candy into their mouths. They sat on the curb in silence, enjoying the sour sweetness, watching another group of kids further down the street.

An owl hooted in the night, loud and close.

They looked at each other, wide-eyed. The two sat motionless, listening. Another owl hooted back in the distance. Jean slid closer to Rob as the two great birds called back and forth.

The haunting night song continued for several minutes and then ended abruptly as a large shadow glided silently out of a nearby tree. It disappeared into the darkness.

"Wow," she whispered.

"That was the coolest thing ever," he said.

She wanted to sit and talk about the owls with Rob, but just then Jean's pack of friends came back down the street.

One of her friends, Courtney, saw Jean sitting on the curb. "Those houses were boring," Courtney said. "C'mon, Jean, let's go around the next block."

She didn't really want to, but her friends were watching her expectantly. It was weird for her to be sitting and talking to a strange boy; she could see that judgment in their faces. She turned and smiled at Rob. "Bye."

"Bye."

Jean didn't see Rob again until the next Halloween. He was an astronaut again, but with a much more sophisticated costume. When he saw her, he looked her up and down just like he had the previous year. "You're a gypsy tiger," he said.

Right again.

She wrapped herself in the precious memory and drifted off to sleep.

When she awoke, hours later, the house was dark. Jean yawned and reached for the lamp next to the chair. She flicked the switch and the bulb flared to life. She rubbed her eyes at the sudden intrusion of light.

She glanced toward the kitchen to get the time from the clock on the microwave but something caught her eye. Her head swiveled back to the entryway.

It took her a moment to figure out what was different, but then the realization pulled the breath from her.

One of the owls was missing from the mirror.

She bolted to the entryway and fumbled for the light switch. The sudden illumination revealed the unmistakable truth—it was gone. The steel surface along the bottom of the frame was smooth, as if nothing had ever been there.

She cried out involuntarily and pulled the bench away from the wall, searching desperately for the missing owl. She picked up the boots and felt inside them with the frantic hope that it had just fallen off after all these years and was lying concealed nearby.

She moved every nearby object and several pieces of furniture that weren't. She found nothing.

It was just gone.

October 29

Sleep evaded Jean for long hours.

She paced back and forth across the house until her feet were sore and then lay on her bed, retracing all the steps of the day. Could Hannah have taken it? No, Jean clearly remembered all four owls being on the mirror after her daughter had left. Even so, she wanted to call Hannah and ask, but backed off the idea quickly. She knew how a frantic late-night call like that would sound, claiming that one of the owls on her treasured mirror had simply vanished into thin air. *Mom has lost it, time to call in the professionals.*

She returned to the mirror and ran her fingers across the bottom of the steel frame. It was as smooth as the glass itself, with no scars or burrs indicating a broken weld.

Jean heard the wind swirling through the trees and rattling the window screens from a sudden gust that continued unbroken for several minutes. A cold front was blowing in, just in time for Halloween.

It all added to the bleak emotions that were building inside her. The house already seemed empty without Rob, but the disappearance of the owl made the silent rooms seem even lonelier.

She padded back to bed and pulled the covers around herself. The chill from outside was already seeping into the house. She tried to relax enough to sleep, but her mind raced from the present to the past and back again.

The common thread in all those transient thoughts was, of course, Rob.

By middle school they had become inseparable. There was just a symmetry between them, a feeling like they'd known each other forever, and maybe even before that. They married five months after graduating from high school, on October 31. Halloween had been their day since the beginning, and making it their anniversary felt like another joyful layer of commitment, a way to perfectly cement a bond made years ago.

As young newlyweds they held raucous Halloween anniversary parties for the first couple years, but then realized they enjoyed the kid-level trick-or-treating aspect of the holiday more, and went out of their way to make Halloween special for the neighborhood children. They constructed increasingly elaborate displays and decorations as they moved from apartment to rented duplex to their own home.

Rob never did make it into space, but he did make it off the ground. He took flying lessons as soon as he saved enough cash, but quickly figured out that if he wanted his own airplane he was going to need a lot more money than anyone in his family had ever possessed. He enrolled in a trade school to learn aircraft mechanics, which at least kept him around airplanes, and after a few weeks of turning wrenches discovered he liked working on planes as much as flying them. It turned out to be a good living.

Jean found work at a local print shop, at first helping customers make copies but soon taking over the production of manuals and brochures for local businesses, along with designing and printing banners and larger displays. That turned out to be a handy talent as their Halloween ambitions grew. The company shifted her to part-time after Hannah was born and for several years thereafter. She had no idea how many millions of pages she had supervised since then. She suddenly felt older than any forty-three-year-old should.

Jean clung to the memories as long as she could before at last reluctantly giving in to sleep. Her fleeting dreams provided no warmth and when she awoke she was still tired. She returned to the mirror immediately, although was not really sure what she was expecting to find. Nothing had changed. The owl had not miraculously flown back to its steel perch while she slept.

I need to get out of the house, she told herself.

She showered and dressed and then hesitantly turned on her phone. She realized it had been powered down for a couple days. The screen came to life with a string of messages from her friends and her sister, with invitations to lunches and dinners and movie nights.

She felt bad for ignoring them and considered calling her friend April to meet for coffee, but April would be at work and Jean still didn't feel up to casual chitchat mixed with well-meaning inquiries about how she was holding up. Especially this morning.

Jean stepped out into pale sunlight and pulled her jacket tightly around herself. She slid into her car, which, like her phone, had been sitting dormant for a couple days, and drove to one of the quieter coffee shops not far from her neighborhood.

Getting away from the house had seemed like a good idea but she passed through the coffee shop like a stranger, locked inside her own mind, smiling distractedly when anyone addressed her.

She sat by herself at a window table and looked outside, her back to everyone else. The coffee was good, but did little to ease the feeling of apprehension she felt.

There was no logical explanation for what had happened.

Was Hannah right? Was a little thing like not putting Rob's boots away a sign of not dealing with reality? She could only imagine what her daughter would say if she went to her with this story of a disappearing owl. Even though the ornamental piece was visibly, *literally*, missing, Hannah would likely be wondering if her mother had removed it somehow and was too distraught to remember doing so. Jean's sister would not be much more sympathetic, she decided, and might even be quicker to drop her off at a hospital.

She finished her coffee more quickly than normal and drove home, a feeling of isolation still weighing her down.

She walked quickly back into the house, tossed her purse down on the bench and almost forced herself to walk past the mirror without looking. But she could not.

She looked. And then stumbled backward.

A second owl was missing from the mirror.

Jean sank to the floor, her back sliding against the door. Her eyes never left the mirror. It was the top owl this time and, just like the other one, there was nothing left to indicate it had ever been there. The steel frame was smooth and unblemished across the top.

She hurriedly pushed herself backward across the cool tiles of the entryway to a corner across from the mirror and table. Her heart pounded with frightening force. She brought her knees up to her chest and wrapped her arms around them.

What the hell is happening?

Jean eyed the two remaining steel owls, half expecting them to fly off on their own. Despite the chill, a trickle of sweat crept across her forehead. She tried to puzzle through an explanation for what was happening, but nothing rational could account for it. She had never really been a believer in supernatural phenomena, despite her fondness for Halloween. She had never seen a ghost, never spied a vampire, never believed in magic. Even now she was reluctant to embrace anything that touched on the otherworldly.

And yet.

She stared at the mirror as if she were an owl herself, unblinking, studying. But the gray surface revealed no clues to what was happening.

She lost track of how long she sat there.

Fear had pushed her into the corner, but the longer she sat, the more she felt a new emotion growing inside her. Anger.

It was a *violation*, this theft of these treasured pieces of her life with Rob.

It got her thinking about actual thieves.

She stood on shaky legs and decided to investigate the house. She went to every room and closely examined all the doors and windows. The inspection revealed no answers. There was no broken glass or ripped screen, no signs of forced entry. Nothing else was misplaced; she checked the other personal items of Rob's she'd kept, but they were all in the boxes and drawers where she stored them.

Jean went to the kitchen and sat at the table. Blades of sunlight were entering through the rear windows now, instead of the front of the house, and she realized with mild surprise that most of the day had already passed.

Her anger cooled and what was left in its place was coalescing into a hard determination.

That's it. No more.

She dragged a chair into the entryway and positioned it across from the mirror. She went to the kitchen, pulled a bottle of water from the refrigerator, grabbed her e-reader and phone and returned to the chair.

"Okay," Jean whispered. "I'm not going anywhere. Come and take another one, if you dare."

She settled in for the long vigil. She plugged the earbuds into her phone and listened to music, but couldn't find anything on her playlist that matched her mood. She switched on her e-reader and began to read, skimming the text for a few seconds, then glancing at the mirror. She did this for a couple hours, barely digesting what she was reading.

It took some time to get her restlessness under control. She sat down on the floor and stretched, banishing the stiffness from her muscles. She paced for a while, but always within eyesight of the mirror.

Daylight faded, giving way to the night. Despite the long afternoon, Jean felt alert and ready, for she suspected that if anything was going to happen it would be under cover of darkness—not that she was turning off any lights.

She returned to her novel, finished it, and began another. As earlier, her attention was divided, and as the hours wore on she realized she was merely holding the device and reading nothing. She was watching the remaining two owls as if she were the mother bird of the nest and they were her fledglings.

It was not until after midnight that the first signs of weariness edged up on her.

Jean rubbed her eyes and took a drink of water. She leaned back in the chair and attempted once more to work through what was happening. None of the options were comforting—losing her mind, or supernatural agents, or hidden intruders in the house. She again wondered what she would say when Hannah questioned her about the missing owls, and that reminded her of the way her daughter's mouth tilted when she was skeptical of something, and that thought meandered to a very pleasant memory of dressing an obstinate Hannah in her trick-or-treating costume when she was four years old...

October 30

She started awake.

It couldn't have been but seconds that she had drifted off and yet she instantly felt the difference in the house.

The mirror stared back at her, mute, three owls gone, only one remaining.

An inner sob coursed through her like a sudden tremor. She thought she might lose control, but the wave of hot emotion passed quickly. She held herself upright in the chair and slowly steadied her breathing and heartbeat. The anger of earlier drifted away.

A calmness descended upon her, and with it, a glimmer of new insight.

She felt no more in control than previously but she had picked up the pattern.

Jean left her perch by the front door and went to her room. She changed into flannel pajamas and crawled into bed.

The last owl wouldn't be going anywhere for a while. Each of the other steel birds had disappeared one day at a time leading up to October 31, like three pages falling from a calendar. It was now early in the morning the day before Halloween. Whatever cruel force was taking the owls would wait one more day before taking the last one. She felt certain about that.

Jean slept late. When she awoke, a fierce hunger reminded her that she hadn't eaten much over the past couple days, so she fixed herself a large breakfast.

As she ate she reflected on the strange limbo that had encircled her life. She had taken the last few days off from work in anticipation of how she might feel on the occasion of her first wedding anniversary without Rob. But she definitely hadn't anticipated *this*.

The eeriness of the missing owls was amplified by the loneliness she felt, and the strangeness of the whole situation kept her walled off from those who might help.

She cleaned the kitchen and got dressed for the day. She made no particular effort to avoid the mirror or focus on it; she had been entirely correct that the fourth owl was still there, and she had no doubt it would remain until tomorrow.

"I'm not going to let you hold me prisoner," she muttered at the mirror on her way out of the house. The fresh air was bracing, and she stood in the driveway for several minutes, eyes closed, letting the cool winds swirl about her. High clouds formed a gray dome above. The feel of the autumn front kicked up pleasant memories associated with the season, lifting her spirits.

She would need whatever strengths she could summon for the next couple of days, she knew, even small ones like this.

Jean opened the garage and loaded a folding chair into the trunk of her car. She settled into the driver's seat and backed out of the driveway, not deciding on her first stop until she was already underway.

She drove to a small florist shop and selected two small arrangements. She placed the flowers on the passenger seat of her car and sat staring at them for some time, before shaking herself out of her trance.

Stop delaying.

She took a deep breath, then pulled out of the florist's parking lot and drove to her next destination.

Pecan Creek Cemetery.

Jean turned off the main road and drove under the stone arch and along the meandering roads that wound beneath the canopy of trees. She tried, with little success, to fight the sinking feeling in her heart that plagued her whenever she visited Rob's gravesite.

She reached the painfully familiar spot near the back and parked along the curb, gathered up the flowers, removed her folding chair from the trunk and walked along the manicured lawn until she reached the headstone that bore her husband's name.

Jean set up the chair then placed the flowers on the grave, one bunch from her, one from Hannah.

She sat quietly for a while, reading the words inscribed on the stone. Twice she started to speak and choked back the words, as if giving sound to the thoughts might reveal them as ridiculous.

She shook her head and finally just let herself speak. "Are you trying to tell me something?" Her voice was soft, barely above a whisper. "Do you need me to do something, or not do something? Are you sending me a warning?"

There was no reply, of course. The world around her was stubbornly normal. She saw nothing that could be interpreted as a sign or portent. Birds darted in and out of the trees as usual. Squirrels hurried across the grass and up the oaks and pecans, gathering material for their winter nests. She looked around and saw nothing but a typical late-October day, warped only by the strange goings-on in her house.

And my mind, she corrected.

"I don't know how to explain to myself what's happening, let alone to Hannah," she said to the plot of earth that held Rob in its eternal embrace. "If you've got any influence over there on the other side, I'd appreciate a little intervention. That's *our* mirror that being dismantled. It's like pieces of me are flying away..." Her voice trailed off, but then an involuntary laugh bubbled up from inside her.

"I gotta say, hubby, if *you're* behind these owls disappearing, you're creeping me out, but *good*." She wiped her eyes. It felt good to joke around like they used to do, even if it was only a one-way conversation.

"You always did know how to read my mood and lift me back into the light. I guess I'll have to do that for myself from now on."

The talking helped. She felt better, but there were no answers here. Whatever was happening, it would just have to play out.

She stood, folded up her chair and carried it back to the car. On the way home she stopped at the grocery store and bought a couple bags worth of food just as if it were any other normal day. Once home, she tried to resume a regular routine. She fixed an early dinner, did laundry and watched some TV, then turned in early.

The fourth owl was still at its usual place on the mirror frame, as she had known it would be. It was not yet its time. Tomorrow, this would end one way or the other, although if events would provide any answers was another question.

"See you on Halloween," she said, and turned off the light.

October 31

When Jean awoke she lay still for a time, just listening to the house. She didn't know what she expected to feel—an intuition perhaps, a sense that something was different. But she could detect nothing out of the ordinary.

She sat up and swung her legs over the side of the bed, tentatively stretched, then stood. The cold hardwood creaked beneath her feet.

Let's get this over with. She grabbed her robe and strode through the house to the front door.

Jean was mildly surprised to find that the final owl was still on the mirror frame. There was even a thin layer of dust on it, she noted with grim amusement.

She still felt certain that the last of the steel owls would take its leave today, but of course had no way of knowing how that process would work. It hadn't happened at the stroke of midnight, or in the predawn darkness, as she might have expected.

"So. Tonight then," she said, running her fingers along the cool metal.

Owls are night creatures. It will be gone after dark.

She resigned herself to a long day of waiting, but the trepidation faded almost instantly. Before this trauma with the mirror she had planned to spend the day remembering Rob, quietly celebrating their Halloween anniversary. Nothing would stop her from doing so now.

Jean got dressed and fixed herself coffee and toast, then went to the spare bedroom where she kept Rob's things. She pulled out the bulky scrapbook she kept in the desk and flipped it open to a random page. She snorted back a laugh. It had fallen open to a Halloween memory, of course. The photos were from the year when the two of them had constructed a large wooden model of an open-cockpit biplane, nearly a third the size of an actual airplane. They'd painted it black with red flames, stuffed a pair of leering plastic skeletons into the cockpit and affixed it to the roof above the garage. Next to it on the page was the clipping from the local newspaper that had run a photo of it.

Jean spent much of the day immersed in the collected pieces of their lives, although, to her surprise, she could not completely lose herself in the memories. She found herself growing increasingly distracted. A growing apprehension crept up on her. It was the prickly feeling that comes with knowing a thing is going to happen, but not when or how.

Irritated at herself, she put the things away. She went to the living room and turned on the TV but quickly felt worse; the act brought on a flush of guilt at wasting time on the anniversary for which she'd so long been preparing herself. Worse, it felt selfish to be watching some stupid show while she'd been pushing away everyone who was trying to reach out to her.

She shut off the TV and turned on her phone. She watched with dismay as the cascade of messages scrolled down the screen. The ones from her daughter had grown increasingly agitated as the hours had piled up with no response. Jean was still not ready to discuss the missing owls, but the prospect of hearing a friendly voice suddenly seemed like a very good idea.

Hannah answered on the first ring, her voice frosty. "Mom. Where have you been?"

"I'm fine. I've just been… running errands."

"Do you want me to come over and be with you tonight?"

"No. I want you to have fun with your friends. I'm going to have one more quiet day to myself. That's all. Just one more day. Let's meet tomorrow for lunch, okay?"

"Promise?"

"Promise."

She sent a couple of quick, short texts to her friends and her sister with more apologies and promises of talking tomorrow.

The rest of the day passed in a haze of anxiety. She tried to ignore the remaining owl, but its presence grew in her mind until it felt like the giant bird was sitting on her shoulder. The waiting dragged on her, until at last the weariness overtook her resolve.

Jean went to the mirror. The frame was smooth on three sides, with the last steel owl still in its customary place. She stared into the glass, trying to read whatever hidden messages might be found in her own face.

"Well, girl, no signs of crazy that I can see."

She lay down on the bench below the mirror and closed her eyes. The rough planks were comforting, something solid and real on a day that felt anything but.

"Please don't take this from me," she whispered, although she wasn't sure whom she was addressing. "I've already lost the man—don't take his gift."

The weak sunlight evaporated, taking with it the last warmth of the day.

She felt a shift then, a barely perceptible change in the world around her, small differences that she would have had trouble describing—a change in air pressure, perhaps, a background noise so faint as to be imperceptible, a hint of static electricity across her skin.

She knew what it meant.

Jean didn't look, but rather reached up with her hand and felt along the right side of the mirror frame.

It was smooth, as bare as the other three sides. The final owl was gone.

She lay still, barely breathing, waiting for the conclusion to play out, for the meaning of it all to reveal itself.

But the world was silent.

Dusk gave way to night. Through her front window she saw the glow from streetlamps as they flickered to life.

She sat up on the bench, rubbing her eyes to hold back tears. She was filled with an aching sadness, but also a frustrating helplessness as events beyond her control dominated her life. At that moment, the lack of an answer bothered her more than the disappearance of ornamental owls.

Jean stepped out on the front porch, hoping the crisp night air would clear her mind. In the distance she heard children laughing as they ran from house to house gathering candy, continuing the Halloween tradition that she and Rob had so cherished.

She looked up into the sky. The clouds had moved off and the stars burned in the night with startling brightness.

"Goodbye, Rob," she whispered to the void. "This was our day and always will be to me. It's a lot colder and lonelier without you."

A new sound rang through the night, a haunting tone of such power and clarity that it cut right through her soul—the hooting call of a large owl.

It was close. *Very* close. She slowly turned her head, trying to spot the bird in the darkness without scaring it off with sudden motion.

It sang out again, and then once more, its deep voice rolling melodically down the street with an all-too-human mournfulness.

Goosebumps raced across her skin.

She saw it this time. Perched atop the utility pole across the street sat an enormous owl, larger than she had ever known possible. Its feathers shone a silvery gray in the starlight.

It leaned forward, puffed out its wings and released a long, low hoot. The sound hung in the air like the ring of a great bell, fading only slowly into silence.

An answering call came from behind Jean.

She spun around and saw an equally large owl on the top of her chimney. Its eyes glowed in the reflected light. The two great birds faced each other and began a halting song, back and forth, the calls twined together in a rhythm born in ages lost in the depths of time.

When the third owl joined the song, Jean spotted it immediately. It was in the upper branches of the tall burr oak in her side yard. Its tone was higher than the others, although it complemented the song of the first two birds with orchestral perfection.

She was expecting it when the fourth great bird called out from a sycamore tree to her left. Jean could see its massive silhouette against the bone-colored branches. Its eyes, yellow embers in the night, glowed from the shadows.

Four owls, all the color of cold steel, all singing in harmony.

Jean walked across her yard until she stood in the exact center of the four owls. All other noises on her street disappeared, as if the nocturnal display had thrown a blanket over other activity. She closed her eyes and let the elemental, feral beauty of the voices wash over her. The timbre of the song was deep and rich, coaxed from a place no human being could fully comprehend. It was as if the owls had taken the night itself and transformed it into an entirely new thing, birthing a song that soared through the air like a living constellation.

Her heart took flight as it followed the rise and fall of the otherworldly birdsong, a chorus at once inspirationally beautiful and achingly sad.

At last she understood what was happening, and the knowledge sent currents of joy and fear through her. This symphony of the owls was an anniversary gift from beyond, from a place so far away she couldn't even imagine.

"Rob?" she whispered in a pleading tone, but even as his name escaped her lips she knew she would never get an answer.

Jean stood enraptured by the great birds, lost in the strange beauty of this impossible gift. They sang until the moon drifted high in the sky, showering the street with cold light. She wanted the song to go on forever, but the calls faded away at last and the four owls departed on silent wings. She found herself standing alone in the moonlight, arms wrapped around herself, holding the song in her mind for as long as she could.

"Thank you, my love. Godspeed."

She walked back into the house, dazed but happy. She closed the door and studied the mirror. It was still bare, and she decided at that moment that she would pack away the mirror where no one would ever see it. The magical gift from Rob would be a secret only the two of them would share. She wasn't sure if she even wanted to know if the owls would come back.

Maybe one day she would look.

THE END

THE GIRL IN THE MIRROR

S. R. BOND

Nothing in this house could be trusted, Grace decided.

As a perpetual foster kid, she'd bounced around from home to home almost constantly growing up. As an adult, she continued the trend—city to city, job to job, apartment to rathole apartment. Renting a bedroom in a beautiful old house in a quaint little town had seemed like a welcome change. Maybe the start of more stability.

The landlord, an elderly woman who insisted on being called Ms. Persephone, was nice enough, but she smell disconcertingly of bleach, and generally ignored her tenant's existence unless Grace was rude enough to ask for something. All of the furniture in the house was pointy and antique—nothing soft or comfortable in sight. It was all as likely to splinter or stab you as to hold your weight.

But the mirror was the worst.

It was old, like everything else in the house, the glass mottled and murky with time. When Grace moved into the bedroom, the mirror was covered by a dusty white sheet. It looked like a ghost lurking in the corner of the bedroom, and it kept her awake at night, so she had pulled the sheet off.

The mirror was six feet tall, towering a half-foot over her head, with a sturdy wooden frame that was plain but obviously well made. The wood was dark and scratched with symbols she didn't recognize, which gave the whole thing a sense of ornate menace.

And she was pretty sure it was giving her bad dreams. They hadn't started until she uncovered the mirror.

Even more disturbing was what she saw when she looked in the mirror.

The first time it happened, she had just woken up from one of the dreams, and she thought she was still asleep. She stumbled out of bed, bleary-eyed, and as she walked past the mirror she caught a glimpse of herself—auburn hair a mess of curls around her head, oversized t-shirt hanging to her knees, brown eyes blinking. But as she looked, the image changed.

It was still her. Or... it still looked like her. But she wasn't hunching through the bedroom in the dark. She was standing straight and tall, her curls bunched into an elegant updo, arms settled gracefully on the wide skirt of a ballgown. The kind of gown you would expect a princess in a fairy tale to wear, she thought. Gold, with thousands of little beads embroidered in swirling patterns of flowers and birds. A wide, low neckline, and a skirt that swept out into an actual train.

She knew it couldn't be real. She must still be dreaming. This was insane, and she refused to be insane. After a moment, when the image didn't fade, she looked closer. The woman in the mirror—this beautiful, poised version of her that she had never seen—stepped closer as well.

Grace stumbled back with a tiny yelp of surprise. When she regained her footing and looked back at the mirror, the image was gone. It was just Grace again, a rumpled mess who had stumbled out of bed in the middle of the night.

And now it was happening again. Not in the middle of the night, so she could pretend it was all a dream, but during daylight hours. It was morning. She had been awake since 6 a.m. Yet there it was, clear as day, her doppelganger in that dress she couldn't imagine ever wearing.

This time Grace decided to be scientific. She moved closer, bracing herself to avoid startling when the girl in the mirror moved toward her, too. She raised her hand and watched as Mirror Girl lifted her hand in return. She twirled, watching in fascination as the skirts of the girl in the mirror twisted and rose as if she was actually dancing.

Tentatively she reached her hand toward the mirror. The girl in the mirror smiled, and nodded.

Grace jumped back, this time with an audible yelp, as her phone buzzed. The girl in the mirror was still watching her, her head cocked to the side curiously.

"Nope," she declared, shaken by the new, unexpected behavior of the Mirror Girl, and tossed the white sheet back over the frame. This was too much. Better a creepy shape in the corner than a mirror that was obviously trying to drive her insane.

Grace glanced at her phone. The text that startled her was from Holly, a girl at her new job trying very hard to crack through her tough shell and befriend her. Holly was a bit too bubbly for Grace's taste, but she didn't know anyone here and she was determined to make an actual life for herself this time.

Waiting outside! The text declared.

Oh *shit*, Grace remembered. She had agreed to go Halloween costume shopping with Holly today. One of their coworkers was throwing a Halloween party tomorrow, and Holly insisted that she had to have a costume or she wouldn't fit in at all.

Well, it would be a distraction, she thought. And Holly was already here.

Be right there, she texted back.

"Later," she muttered, looking at the now-covered mirror. "Later, we're having a serious conversation about how you're messing with my head."

***

Holly was a short, bubbly blond, a tornado of curvy confidence. She had made it her mission to make Grace feel welcome since the day she had arrived as a new secretary in the local law office—the only one in town—and despite Grace's naturally prickly exterior, she had not been deterred.

"Gracie!" she called as Grace stepped outside. "Hurry it up, girl, we've got shopping to do." She shot a grin as Grace smiled tentatively and ran to Holly's bright blue sports car.

Grace had always been uncomfortable with small talk, but Holly talked enough for both of them, babbling about parties, gossiping about people at work, telling stories about random people in town as they drove by them.

She found it comforting to be able to sit back in the passenger seat and tune out a bit. Holly didn't need a response to her conversation—she seemed to enjoy talking for the sake of talking—so Grace listened with one ear but focused her brain on the problem of the mirror.

Before she knew it, Holly was pulling into a parking spot on the main drag downtown, where a row of cute little shops sat quietly waiting for them. This was a small town, but even for the size, the street and shops seemed empty. Too quiet for a Saturday afternoon.

One of the shops sold costumes, and that was why Holly had dragged her out here. Grace had insisted that buying a pre-made costume was too expensive for her budget, but Holly had cajoled until she gave in. This was a new shop, one that had just popped up a few weeks before, and Holly was excited to try it. Besides, Grace's apparent new friend told her, the shop rented costumes, too, and that was bound to be cheaper.

Grace's mind was still on the mirror as they walked into the tiny shop. A bell chirped as Holly pushed open the door with her usual enthusiasm, and a swirl of dust filled the air as the girls walked in. Grace took in the racks of colorful, musty costumes with only a little bit of interest as Holly walked ahead of her, occasionally pulling out something pink or sparkly before tossing it back.

Grace half-heartedly pulled out a generic superhero costume, feigning interest in the red cape hanging limply off the back, before returning it to the rack. The shop was small, like all shops, in the area, but there were a surprising number of racks for such a tight space. Just enough room to move between them through the store, with slightly odd-smelling costumes rubbing against you.

Holly had managed to get a few racks ahead of Grace and was pulling out a sparkly black leotard with a tail and cat ears attached. She added it to a small pile of options hanging over her arm, then motioned that she was heading to the dressing room. Grace nodded and headed that direction as well. As she walked by the final rack in the row, she felt a short, sharp pain, like something had shocked her.

"Ow!" she muttered, rubbing her arm. She looked to her left, frowning, wondering which of these stupid costumes had been laying in wait, ready to hit her with static electricity.

That's when she saw the dress.

The dress. *Her* dress. It looked old, older than anything else in here, and more muted than she remembered it in the mirror. But it was most certainly her dress. Gold, with beaded embroidery running down a full skirt, train pinned up against the back to prevent it from dragging on the floor.

The world spun for a moment as she tried to process what she was seeing. Was she having some kind of episode? Some kind of weird deja-vu? She thought she remembered reading somewhere that serious deja-vu meant you were having a stroke. Maybe she needed to go to the hospital. She definitely needed to sit down.

Grace dropped into a chair outside the dressing room. The edge of the dress peeked out at her from the mass of clothes on the rack, taunting her.

She could hear Holly chattering away in the background, but the words jumbled through her head like the mindless babble of a brook. Nothing about this was making sense. Surely this was not the same dress, but she had seen it so many times now in the mirror, and in her dreams... it was hard to believe there wasn't a connection.

With a deep breath, she stood and walked back to the dress. She reached out an uncertain hand and touched it. Nothing. No burst of static, no sudden visions, just a musty old dress with some pretty gold beads.

It was a relief, but Grace still felt on edge. She tried to refocus on the world around her and ignore the dress, but she couldn't seem to walk away.

"Oooo, that's pretty! You should try it on!"

Holly had come up behind her, wearing the "cat" costume, if it could be called that, and was looking at the dress.

"Um," Grace said smartly. "I can't really afford..."

"Oh, who cares? Just for funsies."

Grace wondered with a cringe how she had ended up with a friend who said "funsies." With apprehension, she watched as Holly reached out and pulled the dress off the rack.

There were no sparks or gasps of pain as Holly touched the dress. She seemed utterly unaffected by it. Cautiously, Grace took the oddly heavy garment from Holly and headed into the dressing room.

It was one of those tiny stalls with a curtain barely covering the front and a cheap, generic, full-length mirror tacked on the wall. Grace stared at the dress for a full minute before she could convince herself to touch it again. No sparks this time, but there was a sense of ominous longing around it in her mind. It felt dangerous and important.

The dress slipped over Grace's head easily. The skirt was heavy and layered, and the weight of it slid to the ground, straightening out the bodice naturally as it fell. The inside was silky and warm, like someone else had just been wearing it, even though she knew it had just been hanging on the rack, untouched.

When she looked in the mirror, Grace didn't see the mature, beautiful girl she'd seen in the mirror at home. It was just her—curls a tangled frizzy mess, brown eyes staring suspiciously at the awkward girl wearing this fancy dress.

It was a beautiful gown. And it fit her perfectly, which was, to be frank, weird. No clothes fit her perfectly. To be fair, she was used to hand-me-downs and thrift store finds, so a well-tailored dress was not something Grace was used to or comfortable wearing.

"Are you going to come out or what?" Holly's voice came through the curtain. Grace imagined she was probably her rolling her eyes in impatience on the other side.

She wasn't sure why, but Grace didn't want anyone to see her in the dress. It didn't feel... right. She reached for the skirt to pull it up and over her head, but Holly was already pulling back the curtain, having reached the finish line of her short attention span.

"Oooo," the other girl cooed. "Super hot. You look like a Disney princess or something."

Grace snorted, trying to push down the butterflies that were suddenly having a party in her stomach. "Whatever. I can't afford it, anyway."

She tried to pull the curtain back, but Holly blocked her. "Well, you need something to wear for Halloween, and this will totally make a statement. How much is it, anyway?"

Grace shrugged, searching for a tag. "It seems expensive," she said, lamely.

"Well, change back, and we'll ask," Holly said. She was being perfectly reasonable, but Grace felt like screaming at her. *Back off,* she thought, teeth gritted as she pulled the curtain closed. There was something like panic swelling in her chest, and she couldn't tell if she was desperate to have the dress or desperate to never see it again.

All she knew was that the dress was waiting for her. That it was made for her.

That was a crazy thought. She grimaced. Back in her street clothes, she felt slightly saner. The dress was just a dress, she told herself. Just a pretty, perfectly-fitted, nausea-inducing dress.

The two women made their way back to the front, where a woman with frizzy gray hair and striking blue eyes was reading a leather-bound book. The very picture of a small-town eccentric, Grace thought with a little smile as the woman looked up.

Her smile faded as the woman stared at her, piercing gaze darting between Grace's face and the dress hanging over her arm. Grace stopped in her tracks and stared back. Something about the woman was familiar, but she was sure they hadn't met before.

"My friend was trying to find a price on this dress," Holly said, oblivious to the tension. She looked at the shopkeeper expectantly, waiting until the woman broke her gaze away from Grace.

"Not a price on that one," the woman replied, setting her book down on the counter. Grace glanced down at the gold lettering on the ancient looking cover. *An Exploration of Alternate Universes.*

Yup, Grace decided. This woman was just plain weird. Nothing to do with her or the dress.

"Do you mean it's not for sale?" she asked. She was almost relieved.

"I mean it's not usually in the store," the woman explained. "If it's here, it's yours."

Holly was frowning. "I don't understand," she said.

The shopkeeper's gaze was on Grace's face again. She was trying to make eye contact, but Grace kept her gaze down. It was uncomfortable.

"Do you remember?" the shopkeeper said softly.

Holly was saying something else, sounding confused, but Grace and the woman in front of her were completely tuning her out at this point.

"Do I remember what?" Grace asked. Her heart was pounding.

The woman smiled. "If you don't know, you don't," she shrugged. "Either way, the dress is yours." She turned back to Holly, motioning her forward to pay for the cat costume, which apparently was not "hers" in the same way Grace's dress seemed to be.

Grace stood stock-still as Holly finished her transaction, then followed her out of the store in a haze. The dress hung heavily over her arm.

As Holly chattered about how weird the shopkeeper had been, Grace sat silently in the car.

Do I remember? She thought. *What am I supposed to remember?*

***

Grace went to bed that night—the night before Halloween—with her mind on the dress now hanging in her closet. She had kept the mirror covered when she brought in the dress. She wasn't quite ready to see what the mirror had to say about it. This was certainly a shabbier version of the dress she'd seen in her vision, or hallucination, or whatever it had been. Then again, she was a shabbier version of that girl, too. And she couldn't shake the feeling that it all meant something.

She didn't get to sleep until after midnight. After what felt like hours of staring at the ceiling, willing herself to stop thinking about the stupid dress and the completely insane mirror, Grace drifted off.

There was a low, gray sense of light when Grace opened her eyes, but she couldn't find the source. She seemed to be outdoors. The ground beneath her feet was silvery and shimmering, textured like sand, and it shifted under her as she took a step forward to take in her surroundings.

To her left, she couldn't see anything but the silver sand, rising and falling in dunes and valleys as it stretched and stretched past her line of sight. To her right, there was more of the sand, with a vague impression of water and lapping waves in the distance.

Not safe.

She felt the words in her head, and she wasn't sure if she heard them or just thought them. There was an impression of wavering air in front of her, sun bearing down on a hot day, and then, without any sound or warning, a woman was standing there.

At least, Grace thought she was a woman. Her hair was long and straight and rippled in a breeze Grace couldn't feel. She kept trying to decide what color it was, or what color the woman's eyes were, but she couldn't seem to concentrate on her face long enough to form a clear impression.

The strangest thing, though, was her wings.

They weren't the wings you would expect from an angel, Grace mused, or even a fairy. She had read plenty of folk stories, and one of her foster homes had mandatory Bible study, so she felt like she had enough knowledge to cover those bases.

This woman's wings were not really wings, she realized, but thousands of butterflies. They were moving constantly, weaving in and out of their comrades, but they never left the formation that gave them the impression of wings on her back.

"Who are you?" Grace finally managed to breathe.

You are not safe, the voice insisted again. *It's time to come home.*

"Home," Grace repeated dumbly. That was a loaded word. She had never really known a stable home, not since she was old enough to have memories. Which, for her, was when she was found wandering the streets at age seven. She had never been able to remember anything before that.

The path will be open tonight, the voice said again. *Come home.* The woman's eyes, which she still couldn't seem to pinpoint for more than a fraction of a second, ran over her face with a deep sadness that chilled Grace to the bone.

"How...?" she started to ask, but—just like that—the woman with the butterfly wings was gone.

And Grace woke up.

***

It was just before dawn. She could see soft light coming in the small single window in the room, casting a hazy glow over everything. In the corner, the sheet-covered mirror loomed, ominous and inviting.

Grace jumped out of bed, throwing on a pair of jeans and a worn t-shirt. She pulled out the ancient laptop that served as her computer and started Googling.

"Mirrors" yielded practically nothing, except a whole bunch of generic mirrors she could buy at various superstores. "Haunted mirrors" was a little more productive—there were several that showed strange images of other people, or gave the owner bad dreams. But nothing quite fit with her experience. She searched "Halloween," since the woman in her dream had mentioned that the "path," whatever that was, would be open tonight. But that just gave her a bunch of websites about superstitions and the history of the holiday, and that was after scrolling past a list of sites selling polyester costumes.

She remembered the book the strange shopkeeper had been reading. On a hunch, she typed in "alternate universes." A list of information on alternate and parallel universes popped up, along with some games and comic book shops. Science had never been her strongest area in school, but as she read she tried to wrap her head around the idea of different universes existing in parallel to each other. Could the girl in the mirror be another version of herself, trying to communicate?

That didn't seem quite right either. The light outside was stronger, and Grace decided she needed to talk to the shopkeeper again.

***

The costume shop was closed. At least, that's what the sign on the door said. It seemed ridiculous that a costume shop would be closed on Halloween. Grace pounded on the door, hoping the woman was inside anyway. No response.

She was about to give up, and in fact had started to walk away, when the door opened.

Grace stared at the woman, who looked at her expectantly.

"I don't remember," she said. "But I want to."

"I can't tell you," the woman replied. "It has to happen in the right time."

Grace snorted in frustration. She was blocking the sidewalk, and people stared in annoyance as they made their way around her.

"When is the right time?" she asked. "Why is the dress important? Why can't I stop seeing myself in it and what the hell is up with the dreams?"

"The dress is important because it comes from your home," the woman said, unfazed by the barrage of questions.

"Home," Grace repeated. "I have no idea where home is. The woman with the butterflies said it was time to go home, and that the path would open tonight, whatever the hell that means. But how am I supposed to go somewhere when I don't know where I'm going?"

The woman's face had gone still. "Woman with the butterflies," she repeated.

"Yes," Grace said. "Like... wings, but just thousands of butterflies. In my dream. She said it wasn't safe."

"Then you'd better hurry," the shopkeeper said. And she closed the door.

Grace knocked again, and yelled, but nothing happened. After ten minutes of unanswered banging, she gave up and headed back to the house she currently called home.

***

After several fruitless hours searching the Internet, Grace decided to get ready for the work Halloween party. After all, sitting around here trying to figure out a puzzle that was missing most of the pieces wasn't doing her any good.

She did her hair and makeup first, stretching out the time before she put on the dress as long as possible. She pushed her curls into an updo as close to the one in the mirror as she could. When she couldn't dawdle anymore, she pulled the dress out and slipped into it.

Like before, it slid over her head like it was made to do so. She left the train bunched at the back for now, not wanting it to drag in the dust that layered the house. Still not willing to look in the mirror in the corner of the room, Grace walked into the hallway to use the bathroom mirror a few doors down.

Ms. Persephone was coming out of her bedroom as she came into the hall. The old woman glanced at Grace, then did a double take. For a moment Grace thought it was because she looked nice, that she was dressed up, but then she saw the expression in the woman's eyes. It was anger. Pure malice, hatred practically pouring off of her in waves. It stopped Grace cold.

"No," Ms. Persephone hissed.

Grace frowned. "Ms. Persephone…" she started.

But the woman had already launched herself at her. She was surprisingly agile for such a stooped, usually slow-moving person, and as she came toward Grace, she could have sworn she saw her yellow nails grow into claws.

Grace stumbled back, barely avoiding being knocked down by her landlord.

"What the…" she started, and then moved back again as the woman went on the attack one more time. Grace cast a wild look around her for options, settled on one of the heavy candelabras sitting on an end table, and dived for it. Ms. Persephone missed her by a few inches and let out an annoyed hiss.

So she was going insane because of a dress and a mirror and now her landlord was trying to kill her. This weekend couldn't get any weirder.

The next time the old woman came toward her, Grace swung the candelabra, hitting her target squarely in the chest. Ms. Persephone—or whoever or whatever she was now—stumbled back, keeping her balance but looking deeply annoyed.

Quickly, Grace ran down the hallway and through the nearest doorway. There were several heavy old pieces of furniture in this room, which was the guest room. They were too heavy to pick up, but Grace moved behind them, putting them in between herself and Ms. Persephone.

The monster that had previously been her landlord—and monster she was becoming, looking more and more like a scary, clawed beast as the minutes ticked by—circled just outside the door of the guest room, slowly making her way inside.

"You weren't supposed to remember," she hissed.

Grace threw up her hands. "I don't," she said. "I don't remember. Let's just calm down and talk."

Calming down did not appear to be on Ms. Persephone's agenda. With an ungodly shriek, she pushed forward again. This time Grace was ready. She had placed herself right in front of a heavy old couch with pointy spires at each low corner—she had poked herself on this particular one in the past—and she stepped aside just as Ms. Persephone threw the weight of her body at Grace.

She missed Grace narrowly and impaled her stomach on the sharp wood. She let out an unpleasant yowl, filled with pain and frustration.

Grace didn't wait around to see what happened next. She darted out of the room and across the hall to her own bedroom, which was starting to feel like a sanctuary.

As she reached the door she felt a sharp pain in her arm. She looked down at the long scratches oozing blood, then back at her snarling landlady, whose face was unrecognizable now. Ms. Persephone's stomach was drenched in black blood. *Not the right color*, Grace thought, feeling a little dizzy, backing up until she hit the wood of her bedroom door.

She struggled with the doorknob, unable to take her eyes off the monster advancing on her, and finally felt it give. She practically fell in as the door opened, but managed to right herself in time to shut it quickly in Ms. Persephone's face.

There was a roar of outrage from outside as she slid the deadbolt into place.

Without a second thought, she ran to the mirror in the corner and ripped off the sheet still covering it. This time, she saw herself as she was—dressed in the gown, hair up. She was a little ruffled from her fight with the monster landlord, and the girl in the mirror still looked perfectly put together. Damn her.

The girl in the mirror was more urgent this time. She didn't waste a moment imitating Grace—she moved closer to the mirror, motioning, clearly wanting Grace to do something.

Grace hesitated only a moment. She had never felt at home. She had never felt like she belonged. What if that was because she *didn't* belong here?

She took a determined step toward the mirror and put out her hand. The Mirror Girl was nodding again, looking pleased. Grace pushed on the glass and felt it give way, rippling out from the pressure she was putting on it. She pushed a little harder, and her hand was gone, through the mirror. She could still feel it, attached to her arm like usual, but she could no longer see it.

Grace felt giddy. She didn't know where she was going, or what would happen, but for the first time in her life she felt like she knew what she was supposed to do.

She stepped into the mirror.

THE END

MAGICK MIRROR

M. G. HERRON

I t was no use arguing with his mother when her mind was made up. Not that Anders always listened to his own advice, of course.

"You need to get out of the house," she said.

"Why?" he asked, eyes fixed forward, hands still gripping a Nintendo controller.

"Because you've been moping for weeks."

"I don't want to."

"I don't care. Now, let's go!"

Anders sighed. He had a different opinion about what he needed to do. He liked the calm dimness of the basement. He liked the bright rectangle of the flat screen TV. He liked getting lost in the story worlds and landscapes of video games. They allowed him to forget, for a time, the nasty breakup with Nadine. Moving pixels on a screen transported him from the fog of melancholy and allowed him to forget that Nadine hadn't spoken more than two words to him in twice as many weeks.

Reluctantly, Anders joined his mother on a short drive to Miller's Bazaar. They parked and strolled down rows of paint-chipped, warped wooden tables that showcased all manner of clothes, produce, gadgets, and other knick-knacks. The late October air was cold enough for scarves. Anders silently protested by refusing a coat.

"I thought you liked this place," Anders' mother said.

"I do."

"Well, cheer up then. This section is just junk and secondhand clothes. I want to go look at the furniture."

Anders groaned. He couldn't bear the agony of browsing battered armoires with her again. She took an excruciating amount of time shopping for furniture. He grasped for an alternative and remembered that Halloween was on Monday.

"I need to get a Halloween costume."

"I thought you said you didn't want to dress up for Halloween this year."

"Ben is. Maybe I can find something here."

"All right." She stepped under the awning and went in a side door of the converted barn. "Don't wander too far."

Anders sighed with relief when she disappeared into the crowd. He turned to tables stacked high with shoeboxes and puffy winter coats. In a tent containing piles of knock-off vintage wear, he discovered several items that might combine to make a convincing Mad Hatter costume—but it was twenty bucks for the Wellington top hat alone, and he'd only brought thirty with him.

Forget costumes, he thought. *Where are the video games?*

Anders stepped into a side door and ambled toward the girls twisting pretzel dough behind a flour-dusted counter. He caught the eyes of a cute brunette about his age. The way she smiled at him reminded him of Nadine's crooked smirk. He blushed and hurried on, wrestling to banish the vivid memories which rose unbidden in his mind: the way Nadine's tank top crept up to reveal the milky curve of her hips and the way she used to wrap her fingers around his in the hall between classes. Anders stalked past the sandwich shacks and barbecue vendors into a crowded area with card and game shops as he fought mightily to shake these thoughts.

Here he slowed his steps and felt a churning in his gut that he recognized as excitement. These vendors mostly stocked out-of-fashion baseball cards and board games, but every once in a while he was able to scrounge up a gem. He had purchased several vintage video games here through the years: *Super Metroid* for the Super NES, *Golden Eye 007* for the 64. He'd even found an Atari 2600 port of *Ms. Pac-Man* from 1984. Never an Atari system that worked, though. Those were rare, coveted by collectors.

"Hey, kid," said an Asian man in a corner stall. He pushed brass wire-rimmed spectacles up on his nose. Anders had never seen him before. "What are you looking for? Baseball cards? Monopoly?"

"Not really my thing. How about video games?"

"Ah, yes. I have Xbox games."

The old man bent down and lifted a heavy plastic bin onto the scratched glass countertop.

"I'm tired of the Xbox. Do you carry any Atari games?"

"Ah, you like the classics. No Atari, but…"

He pushed the plastic bin aside and produced a shoebox from which he reverently lifted the cardboard lid. It was filled with old Nintendo and Super NES cartridges, some in their original (if battered) packaging.

"Swe-e-e-t!" Anders said. "How much?"

"Depends."

Willing to haggle, Anders left the pricing for a later discussion. He flipped through the cartridges, reading the names on their faces and checking them against the mental list he kept of his collection at home. *"Yoshi's Island*, got it. *Mega Man X*, got it. *Super Mario World*, got three of 'em. *Final Fantasy VI*! Awesome. I don't think I have that one."

At the back, he found one in its original packaging. The name was so faded he could barely read it. Then he realized that the letters were Japanese.

Anders lifted it out and flipped the package over. Printed in the bottom right corner below the Japanese letters was the copyright and date, "© 1999 Nintendo." The cover pictured a blonde princess in a revealing dress. A scaly red dragon roared over her, backed by a legion of ghosts and ghouls. In the center, a boy with spiky hair stood alone, wielding an oblong crystal.

"What's this one?"

"Ah. That is *Magick Mirror*."

"Huh. I've never heard of it before."

The clerk took the game from Anders and translated the description on the back for him. "It says, 'released for the first time in Japan… only a hero brave and true of heart can face his fears and defeat the dragon within.'"

Anders frowned. "That's weird, the Nintendo 64 was released in 1996. You'd think they would have made this game for the 64 instead."

The old guy shrugged and pushed his glasses up on his nose. "For you, special price! Fifteen dollars each…buy two get one free. Then you'll find out what it means, true of heart."

Anders nodded. He liked this guy. "Sure. I'll take that one, *FF6*, and *Tetris*."

Spending his cash on video games seemed like a much better bargain than buying a costume he would only wear once. He carried his prizes outside into the brisk autumn air, feeling light on his feet for the first time in weeks. Now, to collect his mom and get home so he could check out the new games.

***

He looked up *Magick Mirror* on IGN.com and all the game-related wikis he could find online, but none had any record of the game. Ben was the master of obscure Internet searches, and he couldn't turn anything up either. Though they discovered that Nintendo continued producing SNES games until 2000, they reasoned that they couldn't find any record of it in English because it was an import.

Anders took the time to locate the Japanese characters and paste them into a search engine. He found a single entry on an obscure vintage game database with a picture of the cover and a translation of the title and description. It was just as the old man said: *Magick Mirror*. An editorial note stated that the game had been released in 1999 and discontinued the following year.

He had stumbled upon a relic. Without further delay, Anders slid the cartridge into the Super Nintendo and flipped it on.

Magick Mirror was an elegant blend of a *Ghouls 'n Ghosts* haunted house button-masher, and puzzle-filled role playing games (RPGs) like *Zelda* and *Chrono Trigger*. Anders was thrilled when he found an English subtitles checkbox in the settings menu. Now he could slay undead monsters *and* enjoy the story.

At its core, the game was a classic romantic adventure—boy meets girl, girl gets kidnapped by evil wizard, boy rescues girl after tromping across the world gathering items, exterminating demons, and unlocking better weapons and armor each time he solved a new puzzle. Unlike most games of its day, the dungeons were surprisingly interactive. Anders spent hours stacking, combining, demolishing, and moving every crate, barrel, and stone gargoyle. Nothing was decorative, nothing superfluous.

No matter how much he leveled his character up, the puzzles required increasing ingenuity to solve. Equipping his newest, most powerful item was never enough; he had to think each challenge through to its logical solution. Anders couldn't imagine why the game had never made it to the States. Even with 16-bit graphics, he was hooked.

By Sunday night, Anders had collected the bronze, silver, gold, platinum, and jade mirrors, and puzzled his way through all five major dungeons using the special skills with which each mirror was imbued. The bronze mirror gave him strength, the jade mirror wisdom, etc. Two hours past midnight, as he was closing in on the princess's location, the story took an unexpected turn: the evil wizard morphed into the scaly red dragon from the cover and absconded with her once again. Anders' character was told that only the crystal mirror was capable of uncovering the dragon's secret lair.

Unlike the previous quests, he was not given any clues to point him in the right direction, and the other non-player characters (otherwise known as NPCs) in the game seemed to be tapped out of helpful hints.

Exhausted from a weekend of gameplay and little sleep, Anders shut off the TV and crawled into bed. His dreams swam with multi-colored mirrors and vermillion dragons, and the princess had Nadine's face.

When he woke, his eyelids felt like anvils. The alarm clock read 5:58. Normally, Anders would stay in bed until his mother dragged him out of it, but the puzzle of the crystal mirror scratched at the back of his brain.

He tiptoed down to the basement and turned on the purple switch that powered up the SNES. On a hunch, Anders went back to the house he started in, and there was the spirit of the good wizard, who had died at the beginning of the game, waiting for him.

Greetings, Anders, read the text, which unfurled across the screen. *I'm glad you found your way home in time. The question is, are you now prepared to wield the crystal mirror?*

A yes/no dialogue popped up. Anders selected *Yes.*

Very good! the wizard responded. *In that case…*

The wizard held up a crystal mirror in his hand, a vaguely ovular piece of glass with pixelated edges angled like a parallelogram. The flat screen of the television warped and wobbled. At first, Anders thought it was an effect of the game, and he was momentarily impressed to see such a vivid rendering on an old console. A moment later the tall, rangy, semi-translucent spirit of the wizard materialized in front of him in the dim light of the basement.

"What the—" Anders lurched from the couch.

"Well done, young Anders!" The tip of the wizard's pointy hat wobbled as he nodded. "Very well done, indeed. I believe this belongs to you now."

Stunned, Anders could do nothing but drop his controller and accept the crystal mirror.

"The crystal mirror's magic ability is insight. It allows you to see that which others do not. With it you can uncover the dragon's lair, drive him from it, and rescue the Princess Nadine."

Anders blinked. "Wait, what?"

"Perhaps you'll find a use for this as well." He removed and held out his tall hat, dark blue and patterned with starbursts. His hair was balding beneath it. "Good luck, noble warrior."

Without another word, the wizard warped, faded, and vanished.

Anders looked down at the crystal mirror, felt its solid weight in his hands.

"Holy shit," he said to the empty basement. "What just happened?"

"Anders," his mother called from the top of the stairs "You're going to miss the bus!"

Anders shook his head, stuffed the artifact into his backpack as he scrambled up the stairs, and bolted through the door without making eye contact with his mother. It was only as the door slammed behind him that he realized he was clutching the wizard's hat in his hand.

***

Anders took the three steps onto the school bus at a sprint. He smiled awkwardly at the driver, who gave him a knowing scowl from behind a mask of green paint. Two metal bolts stuck out of his temples.

Anders panicked as the bus lurched forward. His breath quickened and his throat went dry. He stumbled his way down the aisle, past his classmates dressed as monsters and ghouls and zombies and witches and—

A tall boy in a black leather trench coat stepped into the aisle. He wore reflective sunglasses and held out two fists toward Anders as he approached.

"You take the blue pill, the story ends. You wake up in your bed and believe whatever you want to believe. You take the red pill, you stay in wonderland, and I show you how deep the rabbit hole goes."

Anders froze. His jaw hung open. His hands began to shake.

"I know, it's perfect, isn't it? I look just like Laurence Fishburne. Hey, take it easy dude. Are you all right? It's me, it's Ben."

Ben helped Anders to an empty seat. Anders struggled out of his backpack, whose weight with the crystal mirror inside seemed to constrict his movement. He put his head between his knees.

"I can't believe this is happening," Anders mumbled, wiping sweaty palms on his jeans. "It's just make believe. It's not real. It's not real."

When he managed to get his breathing under control, he zipped open his pack and removed the smooth crystal, which looked more like a large piece of cut glass than a traditional mirror.

He ran his fingers along its edges. The object was real all right.

"I didn't mean to freak you out, man," Ben said.

"It's okay," Anders said. "Not your fault. Nice Morpheus costume."

"Is this your wizard hat?"

"Yeah."

"Sweet." Ben picked up the hat and stuck it on Anders' head. "Where's the rest of the costume? No robes? A magic wand? A spellbook?"

"Uh..." Anders lifted the crystal mirror in his hand. "Just this."

"Neat. What is it?"

"Listen, you remember that game I told you about, *Magick Mirror*? Well you'll never believe this... I barely believe it myself, to be honest... but *this* is the crystal mirror from the game."

"Sick! You didn't tell me it came with a replica."

"No, it's not a replica. I mean it's actually from the game. This morning, the spirit of the good wizard appeared in my basement—"

"Hi, Ben." A cat poked her nose over the back of the seat. "I like your costume."

"Thanks, Lucy. Yours is rad, too. What kind of cat are you supposed to be?"

"A Siamese. Elizabeth is dressing up as my twin. We coordinated last week."

Ben patted Anders' shoulder as he slid out of the seat they shared and in next to Lucy.

Anders sighed and gazed down at the crystal in his hands. He could see through it to the brown floor of the bus below. *If Ben doesn't believe me*, he thought, *no one will*.

As Anders turned his thoughts inward, the crystal's surface clouded with mist. The tendrils slowly solidified into a 16-bit sprite of his own self, dressed like the hero in *Magick Mirror*. In the top left corner, four red hearts appeared—just like in the game. Any doubt as to the artifact's reality instantly evaporated.

His character turned back into mist and the mist formed wispy words, which read, *The crystal mirror's ability is insight. Focus through the glass to activate it.*

Anders looked around. No one else seemed to be paying attention to the incredible magic he held in his hands. Pulled by a bright sense of wonder, Anders turned in his seat and held the crystal mirror in front of his eyes.

"Sup, Merlin?" Ben asked.

"Just…testing a theory," Anders said. Through the mirror, Ben could be seen not wearing the Morpheus costume, but transformed into a dashing adventurer, dressed in rugged browns and greens topped with an Indiana Jones hat. He gazed down at a map in his hands, and the map was marked with crisscrossing dotted lines leading to a bold X, which shined out of the parchment and reflected in Ben's glasses.

One side of Anders' mouth quirked into a smile. "I always knew you were a man of adventure, Ben. You're destined for great things."

A grin lit Ben's face. "Right on!"

Anders shifted the crystal mirror so that he could see Lucy through it—and gasped when a boil-faced witch glared back at him. In his surprise, Anders fumbled the crystal mirror and heard it thunk to the floor of the bus.

Ben guffawed and covered his mouth. Lucy's nose scrunched up. She scowled at Anders as she stood from her seat. "Screw you, Dumbledork! You're a real jerk."

She climbed out of the seat over Ben.

"Dude," Ben whispered. "That was hilarious."

"Heh. Yeah?" Anders managed to reply. He bent under the seat, retrieved the mirror, and stuffed it back into his pack.

For the rest of the ride, Anders sat in silence and stared into space while his mind raced to decipher the mirror's meaning. In a way, it made a lot of sense. The mirror's power was insight, and the images it had shown him had been insightful in their own way. Ben really did have a great sense of adventure. Anders had known it since the moment they'd met in elementary school and bonded over their mutual love for all things nerdy, whereas Lucy and Anders had never gotten along. Even now, she was no doubt whispering venomous thoughts to her friends while plotting a dubious revenge against his insensitivity.

Anders turned around to explain his theory to Ben, but he had switched seats again to flirt with Lucy and her friends.

Anders decided to stash the crystal mirror in his locker and figure out what to do with it later. In school, as he turned down the hall to his locker, he spotted Nadine, wearing a pleated blue skirt. Her hair was divided into twin golden ponytails. His body's response to her short, body-hugging Sailor Moon costume made him jerk back around to hide both his groin and his red face. He cursed under his breath.

When he turned back into the hall and hurried to his locker a moment later, he caught a look of Nadine in his peripheral vision and his heart clenched in his chest. *What a knockout! How did I manage to screw it up so badly with someone like her?*

He pretended to busy himself in his locker while Nadine opened hers a few feet away to stash a binder. She closed the metal door, hesitated a moment, then turned away.

Unable to resist, Anders held the crystal mirror before him and looked at Nadine's retreating back. A delicate golden tiara on her head sparkled under the fluorescent lights.

Boyd Bohannon stepped out of a side hall and slid up next to Nadine. Boyd was a stereotypical jock, and today he wore a Peyton Manning jersey for his "costume," with a gym towel around his neck. He had birds for brains, of course, but all the girls swooned over him. It drove Anders crazy.

He felt his lips twist into a sneer as he anticipated what came next. He shifted the mirror to focus on Boyd.

What he saw gave him the worst shock of the day. Instead of being the evil wizard/dragon who had stolen the princess, as Anders suspected, through-the-glass Boyd was a bespectacled doctor in a white lab coat and stethoscope.

"Seriously?" Anders muttered.

His guts twisted up like a Gordian knot. Somehow, it was easier to think of losing Nadine to Boyd when he was just a dumb jock. But Boyd as a good guy, a doctor no less? The thought was unbearable.

Anders took a step forward to chase after Nadine. He wanted to pull her aside and make a loud declaration of his everlasting love for her, to say everything he'd been too embarrassed to say to her before.

As before, he failed to summon the courage. Instead, he sighed and turned away with a dry, dead taste like ash on his tongue. As he opened his backpack to stash the mirror, his sprite took a punch to the jaw and fell down, a certain metaphor for his inaction.

A heart dropped off his life gauge, and he was left with three.

***

Anders zoned out through his next two periods while his mind turned over this new puzzle. He began to think of it as the IRL—"in real life"—game. The most frustrating thing was that no more instructions appeared in the crystal. Just the three hearts he had remaining and, if he looked into its surface while his thoughts were turned inwards, himself as a 16-bit sprite.

Because it was Halloween, Anders walked the halls and sat in class with the mirror in plain sight without anyone looking at him sideways. He even managed to sneak a few glimpses of his teachers and classmates through it. What surprised him most was that almost no one appeared the same way they presented themselves in person. One shy girl who had a nervous habit of chewing on the ends of her hair and who had not worn a costume, perhaps out of shyness, was decked out as a glamorous singer with pink punk rock bangs. Meanwhile, his stressed-out computer science teacher, Mr. Roy, who had worn a flannel shirt to match his glue-on lumberjack beard, appeared through the glass as a smooth-flying pilot, with a scarf around his neck and aviator goggles affixed to his face.

The bell marking the end of third period rang, and students rushed out on their way to lunch. Eager to test the mirror's magic on a less intimidating target than Nadine, Anders slowly packed his things and waited until the rest of class had filtered into the hall before he rose from his seat.

"Mr. Roy?"

"What's up, Anders? Did you have trouble with the lab?"

"No, that was actually pretty easy. I…ah…wanted to ask you about something else." He paused, unsure how to phrase it without seeming like he was prying. He settled on a version of the same question adults had been asking him for years: "What did you want to be when you grew up? You know, when you were my age?"

Mr. Roy scratched the grey hairs at his temple. "Oh, boy. No one has asked me that in a long time."

"I'm just curious."

"I don't mind telling you: I wanted to be a pilot."

"You should do it," Anders said, surprised at the conviction in his own voice. "Really. You'd be a great pilot. Goggles on, wind blowing in your face. Isn't that what you always wanted to do?"

Mr. Roy's lips parted and closed again. Reluctantly, he nodded. "Pretty dated description of a pilot, but yeah, it really was. Life doesn't always turn out how you expect."

"Tell me about it. You should do it anyway. Get your pilot's license or something. It's never too late."

Mr. Roy smiled sadly. "Thanks, Anders. I appreciate that."

"Sure thing. See ya later, Mr. Roy."

As he strolled out of the classroom, Anders looked down at the mirror. Mist swirled and formed the letters: *Bonus! +200.* The two hundred points moved to a new counter in the top right of the crystal next to a coin icon. Anders smiled and quickened his pace to the cafeteria.

After standing in line for lunch, he slid into a bench at a long table next to Ben, who was deep in a heated discussion with Marcus and Geoff about *The Matrix.* Anders was waiting impatiently for a break in the conversation when Nadine and her friends sat next to them at the long table.

Anders glanced around. The cafeteria was crowded. Boyd squeezed into the bench next to Nadine.

Anders pushed two french fries around his tray with a fork while he tried not to pay attention to Nadine sidling up next to Boyd. After an anecdote about freshman hazing rituals among the football team, at which Nadine and her friends giggled uncomfortably, Boyd reached up one tan arm and rested his wrist on Nadine's shoulder. Anders clenched the plastic fork in his hand so hard it broke in half. The loud snap caused everyone to look at him.

Nadine shrugged out of Boyd's embrace.

Boyd turned on Anders. "What's your deal, twerp? You got a problem?"

"Boyd, don't," said Nadine.

Riled up by the very fact that Nadine would try to rescue him from Boyd's imbecilic wrath, Anders responded hotly, "You're like a lodestone for intolerance. Does it make you feel like a man to fill freshman lockers with shaving cream, or do you just get really excited sniffing their jockstraps?"

"You little shit!" Boyd lunged across the table. Anders dodged out of Boyd's exceptional reach, and then danced back from the table.

"Stop it, both of you!" Nadine cried. Boyd pushed himself to his feet and stood there, his shoulders heaving.

Anders caught Nadine's eyes for a brief moment. She scowled at him and stormed out of the cafeteria. Boyd glared at Anders before chasing after her.

Anders gazed down at the crystal. His heart count had been reduced to two.

***

Ben walked with Anders to Mrs. Werner's Honors English class. They took their seats and spoke in whispers as their classmates drifted in.

"Damn, A, you've got some balls of steel today," Ben said. "You're lucky Boyd is too thick to get into an Honors classes or we'd both be ground beef."

"You'd stick up for me against him?"

"You know I would."

"Thanks, Ben. But it's not that I've got balls of steel, it's that this crystal mirror is freaking me out. Everything I've seen in it is true."

Ben's easy-going smile deepened into a frown. "What are you talking about?"

"You've gotta see it to believe it." Anders handed the mirror to Ben. "Look through it at anyone in here and concentrate, then tell me what you see."

Ben aimed the crystal at Mrs. Werner. "I see…a boring lecture about Odysseus coming our way!"

Mrs. Werner scowled at Ben. He shifted so he could see Anders' face through the glass instead.

"Do you see it?" Anders asked.

"See what? I just see you in that goofy wizard hat."

Anders groaned. "Give it to me," he said. He took the mirror back, and when he gazed into it the mist had formed new words, flashing red: *No cheating.*

The little hairs on the back of his neck stood on end. When he fell silent, Ben shrugged and turned away.

The admonishment seemed to defy the standard rules of RPGs. All reluctant heroes were allowed to gather their party to help them in their quest. If anyone fit the role of sidekick, it was Ben. How was asking his best friend's advice considered cheating?

Then Anders remembered: once he had been tasked with acquiring the crystal mirror within the game, the NPCs had become reticent and quit giving his character hints and suggestions. Like the hero of *Magick Mirror*, Anders was left to wrestle with this challenge on his own.

He brooded over his dilemma for the rest of English class. The questions brought on by the implied game rules he'd learned so far seemed endless. What would happen to Nadine if he lost all his hearts? How was he supposed to find the dragon's lair and rescue her? And if Boyd was *not* the evil wizard/dragon, then who was?

One thought depressed him the most: if he lost all of his hearts, then what would happen between he and Nadine? Would it mean he had finally blown any last chance of getting back together with her after all?

He spent the next period and as much time in the hall between classes sneaking glances at as many of his peers as possible, looking for any sign of the beast or its hideout. He found none, and when he walked into last period, Ms. Bozeman told him to "put the toy away." He finally gave up and stashed the mirror once more.

Ms. Bozeman taught Algebra II, and she was good at it. Because of her skill as a teacher, and the way she refused to take crap or excuses from any of her students, it was one of the few classes Anders actually enjoyed attending.

Ms. Bozeman was dressed as a pirate wench, albeit a classy one. A striped bandana tied down her greying brown hair, and a leather vest was laced up the front of her white blouse. Beneath the poofy petticoats, Anders could see that, sensible as always, she had worn black tennis shoes.

Anders gazed at Ms. Bozeman through the mirror and was delighted to see that she looked like a hippie version of her non-Halloween self. Her clothes were tie-dyed and her horned glasses groovier, but her shirt was still dusted with chalk around the stomach. Unlike almost everyone he'd seen through the mirror, Ms. Bozeman was exactly what she meant to be. She had found her true self.

Anders lowered the mirror and hurried to his seat when Nadine entered the room. This was the one class they shared, last period. He spent the class focused on the blackboard and his notepad, with occasional glances at the mirror in his lap to check his heart count, refusing to look in her direction.

He made it to the end of the school day without losing any more hearts. When the bell rang, he even managed to be the first one out the door.

Outside in the parking lot, Anders let his mind wander. *What could be done to reverse the effects of the game? Take out the cartridge? Reset the console?* He was willing to try anything. Maybe it would work.

Someone tapped his shoulder. Turning, his stomach dropped into his feet. He looked straight into Nadine's big green eyes.

"Hi," she said.

"Uh," he said. "Hi." *Stupid, stupid, stupid.*

"Are you okay? You're acting weird."

"No, it's...I'm fine, totally fine, yeah. How are you?"

"Really? Can you just be honest with me for *once*, Anders?"

He felt his face flush with shame. The crystal began to slip out of his sweaty fingers. He shifted it to his arm and held it like a heavy tome in the crook of his elbow.

"Boyd is a douchebag." The words slipped out before he could stop them. "He doesn't deserve you."

"You don't know him. He's a nice guy."

"Please, he's only nice to you because you're pretty."

"At least he talks to me."

Anders stared at his feet.

"That's it?" she asked. He looked up at her beautiful face. He loved the way her sharp chin wrinkled when she was concerned about something, the way she puckered her lips, to which *just* the right amount of lip gloss had been artfully applied. These reminders wrenched at his heart. They forced his thoughts back to a month ago, when her attitude toward him had been different, when the temperature of the air between them had been less frosty.

For once, he said what he was really thinking: "You want to know the truth? The truth is that I want you back."

Nadine's brow scrunched and she shook her head. "First you don't say anything…and then we don't talk for weeks, and now you want to get back together? Are you serious?"

"Yes! It's the only thing that makes sense. We have to get back together."

"Anders…I don't…I can't. I just can't."

"Nadine! Wait!"

She turned and ran to the front of the school, pushing through the crowd of people swarming toward the bus.

Anders held the mirror out and gazed after her retreating figure. He lost another heart. Though he couldn't find the beast in the crystal, Anders knew that a dragon had stolen Nadine from him again.

***

Anders thudded down the basement steps and fell to his knees in front of the Super Nintendo. The *Magick Mirror* cartridge was inserted in the console exactly as he'd left it.

He turned on the TV and pushed the purple power switch forward.

Nothing happened.

Anders removed the cartridge and blew the dust out of it like a harmonica, clearing the circuitry of debris. He shoved the cartridge back into the console and shifted the power button to *On* again.

A brief flash brightened the television screen, and then nothing.

Clenching his jaw, he rummaged for the mirror in his pack and set it on the floor. The surface flashed red mist-letters at him when he tried the button a third time. *Not allowed.*

He pumped the reset button instead. *Nice try*, the mirror read.

"Aw, c'mon, are you kidding me?" He cursed, tore the rare cartridge from the classic console, and threw it against the brick wall. It bounced unharmed to the thin carpet.

Anders picked up the mirror and used it to smash the cartridge into the floor. Pieces of plastic and circuit board hopped and scattered with each blow. When the cartridge had been pulped sufficiently to make smashing it no longer satisfying, Anders lifted the console over his head—the Super Nintendo Entertainment System which had gifted him with his earliest remembered sense of wonder and thousands of hours of entertainment—and hurled it against the wall over and over and over, his chest heaving, his eyes flooding with tears of rage, his hoarse screams of frustration echoing through the damp basement air.

When the console was annihilated, Anders lifted the crystal mirror with a grim expression and pitched that, too, against the brick wall. It bounced off without a dent.

Breathing heavily, he brought the crystal upstairs to the garage. He dropped it in the middle of the smooth cement floor and retrieved his father's sledgehammer.

He squared his legs like his father had taught him, pulled the hammer back over his head, and brought it down with all his might. The hammer clanged like a great bell. His hands tingled with the aftershock that traveled down the handle.

As if to mock him, the surface of the crystal mirror wobbled with the impact, but remained unblemished.

He pulled the hammer up, gritted his teeth, and brought it down again. And again. And again. His hands went numb and shook from the exertion. Eventually, his shoulder muscles reached their limit. The sledgehammer slipped to the floor, and Anders collapsed onto the cold cement.

He covered his head with his arms and lay there, completely still except for his labored breathing. Normally, he treasured this gap of time between school and when his parents got home from work. Without a reset button for his life, and no way to beat the insane game he had been forced into, his freedom felt like a sham. He was stuck in the black mineshaft of his own bitter soul, and not even a sledgehammer could bust him out.

Anders wiped the sweat from his brow. He felt like he'd been run to ground, but more clear-headed following the physical exertion. One thing was certain: there was no reset button, no going back. He had to see the game through to its end. Even if he lost. *Especially* if he did.

He had fallen in love with *Magick Mirror* over the course of the weekend, and now the quirks of the game began to return to him. He was reminded how ahead of its time the game was, how incredibly interactive the 16-bit dungeons. He remembered how it was never the newest item, never the mirrors, which helped him solve the puzzles—the artifacts were merely tools, used to gain access to the dungeons. Once inside, you were left to use your own cleverness to get the treasure and escape unharmed. He chuckled when he recalled how he'd spent an hour after finding the bronze mirror hurling barrels and rocks against the puzzle in the first dungeon, and how the solution he eventually found had nothing to do with the super strength the bronze mirror bestowed. All he had to do was arrange the barrels and boulders in a pattern matching the arrangement of boulders and barrels on the barred-off side of the room, and *voila*! He was in.

Why, then, had he been so foolish as to think trying to smash the crystal mirror was ever going to work? The puzzles could only be solved by using the clues that he had been given.

Anders didn't gasp when the realization hit him, but he quit wallowing in his own remorse. He stood, scooped up the mirror, and went to his computer. Fortunately, he hadn't considered trashing *that* piece of expensive electronics. He navigated to the bookmarked page on *Magick Mirror* and reread the description from the back cover translated on the website. '*Released for the first time in Japan, this clever mashup of haunted houses and puzzle-based RPGs is not for the faint. Only a hero brave and true of heart can face his fears and defeat the dragon within.*'

That's what the man at Miller's Bazaar had told him as well. The clue had been staring him in the face all along!

He shut the laptop, pulled his bike out of the garage, and aimed it toward the west side of town where Nadine lived.

***

Anders dropped his bike at the edge of the Mr. Mortimer's property. The house was a light blue Cape Cod with bay windows and a wraparound porch.

Through the lens of the crystal, which Anders raised and brought close to his face so as to get a full view of the truth of his world, Nadine's house appeared not as a quaint suburban homestead, but as the mouth of a great cave rent asunder beneath a burnished orange sky. The beautiful sunset was real enough. Only, through the crystal, trails of smoke twisted into the air.

He had found the dragon's lair, with one heart remaining.

He thought about throwing rocks at Nadine's window but, considering the use of the word *'brave'* in the game's description of its hero, decided against it. Anders approached the front door instead, holding the crystal like a shield.

Shaking despite himself, Anders reached up and rapped the brass knocker three times.

After an agonizing moment, Nadine's mother opened the door. She glared down her nose at him.

"Anders," she said. "What do you want?"

He cleared his throat. "Hi, Mrs. Mortimer. Can I please speak to Nadine?"

"She doesn't want to see you."

Anders nodded and stared at the whitewashed boards of the porch. The *Welcome to Our Home!* mat seemed entirely too cheerful for this moment.

He lifted his chin and looked Mrs. Mortimer in the face. "I understand. I made a mistake. I just need to apologize to your daughter and then I'll leave."

She crossed her arms and cocked her hip to the side. Then she sighed. "All right, fine. But I'll be right here. Listening to *every word*. And if you hurt her again you will regret it, young man. And I mean it. She doesn't deserve that kind of treatment."

"Yes, ma'am," Anders managed to mumble.

Mrs. Mortimer clucked her tongue and turned away.

As she turned, Anders brought the crystal up and looked at her as she walked away. She wasn't the dragon, though. He saw Mrs. Mortimer as a lean, sinewy lioness, a mama cat protecting her baby cub.

A moment later, Nadine came out. With the mirror held before his eyes, Anders saw her through it, too. She still wore the cute sailor moon skirt, and she looked exactly like herself through the crystal, except for the shining tiara.

He dropped his arm as Nadine approached.

"What's your deal with that thing?" she said

"It's a magic mirror. Its power is pure insight. You look through it and it shows you what a person is really like on the inside."

"Let me see," she said.

Nadine took the mirror and held it up to his face. "Ah, yes," she said. "I see a selfish jerk who only cares about his own problems."

A chill swept over his body when he thought, for a moment, that Nadine was really seeing him with the mirror. That its magic had actually worked for her. He barely stopped himself from turning away and retreating to his basement where it was dark and safe. Then he remembered how the mirror's magic hadn't worked for Ben, and how retreating into the fictional universe of video games hadn't helped him deal with any of his problems, either.

Instead, he swallowed the lump in his throat and managed to whisper, "I deserved that."

He lifted his face to hers and noticed that Nadine's eyes were bloodshot like she'd been crying. This whole time, through the last month of their mutual silence,

Anders had made the foolish mistake of thinking he was the only one who had been effected by the way their relationship had ended. She put on such a brave face at school. Now he knew how wrong he'd been.

And in that moment, he knew where the dragon was hiding.

He gently took the mirror from Nadine's hands, looked into it, and concentrated. For the first time, the surface turned to solid silver and reflected back his own image—the steaming snout of a toothy, terrible dragon.

He was the dragon.

Or, more accurately, his own fears and misconceptions were. He knew what he had to do.

"Listen, I don't know why I brought this," Anders said. He turned to the open door and chucked it into the lawn. "I just came to say how sorry I am about...the way things ended. I'm really, really, really sorry." He took a shaky breath. "I was too embarrassed about...you know...to say anything. I tried to, but I just couldn't. And then I saw you with Boyd—"

"I keep telling him to keep his hands to himself but I swear we never—"

"Really?"

"Really really."

He was about to say "it doesn't matter," but he realized it did. Nadine glanced over her shoulder, ushered Anders onto the porch, and closed the door behind them.

They sat on the porch steps while Anders gathered his courage to continue. "I tried to tell you, but Boyd was around all the time and it seemed like it was too late to tell you how I really felt. It's impossible to have a private conversation at school or"—he glanced at the closed door behind him—"or anywhere really. You're always surrounded by your friends, or with Boyd, or in class. I just got so frustrated. And then before I knew it, it was too late to say anything at all."

"Oh, Anders," Nadine said. "I thought you didn't...like me anymore."

"What! Are you kidding? Have you seen yourself in this Sailor Moon costume? How could anyone not like that?"

She laughed, a beautiful sound like a wind chime, and then snorted and covered her mouth with her hands.

"I love your laugh so much," he said.

Anders saw *Bonus! +1000* fly across the surface of the mirror in the grass. He forced down a smile.

"Really? It's so awful..."

"Awfully cute."

She smiled shyly. They sat in silence for a moment.

"So, are you seeing Boyd now, or...?"

Nadine picked at the paint on her toenails before answering. "We went to the movies a couple times. I don't know. I guess."

Anders fought to keep his voice steady. "All right then. Well, I'm happy for you, and that's all I had to say. I guess I'll see you later."

She grabbed a handful of his t-shirt as he stood. "Don't be silly," she said. "Stay a little while."

He sat back down. She rested her head on his shoulder and intertwined her fingers with his.

"What did Boyd think of your Sailor Moon costume?" Anders asked.

"Ugh...he thought I was dressed up as a cheerleader."

"No way!" Anders said, chuckling. "Is that why you were mad at him at lunch?"

"I'm not mad at him. We just don't have much in common. I bet *you* knew I was dressed up to be Sailor Moon for Halloween."

"Instantly."

They talked about everything and nothing until the sun set. Long after the streetlights came on, Anders reluctantly disengaged his fingers from hers.

"My parents are probably worried," he said. "I should go."

"Okay."

"We should hang out this weekend."

"Want to go bowling at Lucky Lanes? Linda said they finally got someone in to fix the old *Ms. Pac-Man* game in the arcade."

"Sounds great."

"All right," Nadine said as she went back inside. "See you tomorrow."

"See ya."

Anders scooped up the mirror from the lawn. At his bike, he turned one last time and gazed at Nadine's house through the crystal mirror. A massive vermillion dragon lay limp and smoking in the mouth of the cave.

***

His mom and dad yelled at him for leaving the sledgehammer in the middle of the garage—apparently his mom nearly drove right over it—but when they realized he'd been at Nadine's house, they forgot all about the tool. His mom offered him dinner instead.

In the basement, the console and cartridge of *Magick Mirror* had been miraculously restored and placed next to a neatly coiled controller. No sign of the destruction he had caused was visible. The crystal mirror was gone from his bag, too. When he booted up *Magick Mirror*, he was rewarded with a scrolling credits screen.

***

Shortly before Christmas break, Mr. Roy announced to Anders' class that he was quitting mid-year to pursue his dream of becoming a pilot. He'd taken a job with a subsidiary of an airline, a stepping-stone that would give him the opportunity to get enough flying hours to become a commercial pilot.

Though they were in separate periods of Mr. Roy's class, Anders and Nadine planned a surprise going away celebration for him. She baked cupcakes with little airplane figurines sticking out of blue and white frosting, and Anders arranged a special viewing of *Top Gun*.

"Thanks for everything, Mr. Roy," Anders toasted him as the movie started. "May you fly high and live your dream!"

THE END

THE ANTIQUE MIRROR

D. F. JONES

Dedication: To my mother, Earlene

Rockvale, Tennessee 2015

"Maybe this wasn't a great deal, after all," Victoria said, talking to herself as she navigated her silver Jeep down the narrow driveway that was in need of serious attention. The driveway seemed to go on forever, until the property finally opened up to a meadow; there it was—the cozy cabin in the woods.

Victoria sucked in a deep breath as she looked around the small farm. Wild daisies were scattered throughout the property and a white picket fence enclosed the small yard. A trellis of roses climbed both rock fireplaces on either end of the cabin. There was a covered front porch with stained glass windows over the door. Tori noticed a small barn with a red, tin roof, and a split-rail fence that ran along the perimeter of the property.

Oh, this was too good to be true. Victoria stepped out of her Jeep and put on her professional smile; it was show time.

At twenty-eight, Victoria Frost was a successful artist in Nashville with her naturalist representations of landscapes and abstract still-lifes. Tori's skillful painting technique created an illusion of texture with bold colors. She had sold nearly all of her big pieces at the Heart and

Soul Gala for Vanderbilt Children's Hospital.

Many local art dealers around the Nashville area had indicated to Max Dupres, Tori's agent, that they would be willing to host fundraisers and galas if she had her own studio and gallery. An art barn would be ideal to rent out for a variety of events while displaying her art for sale.

Tori had been dreaming of a place like this to work, hike and be at one with nature. Hell, she might even buy a dog.

The Realtor nearly crushed Tori's fingers with his handshake. "Victoria Frost, I'm Andy Crenshaw, Crenshaw Realty. So glad you found it. There was another couple who just left here and they loved the place."

Oh, please, not that old sales ploy. "My friends call me Tori and if someone else is interested, I'll go. There's another property in Leaper's Fork I'm looking at this afternoon." Tori turned to leave. Her inner diva was doing a fist pump.

Andy stepped around in front of her and hastily replied, "Ah, now Tori, surely you'll take a look around the property while you're here. The couple was interested, but I don't think they'll qualify for the loan."

Tori turned and entered the cabin. She stood in the foyer for a few minutes to get a feel for the place. There was a gorgeous antique chandelier hanging overhead. Two huge rooms flanked either side of the foyer, and each had a rock fireplace with oak mantle. The corners of the mantles had been carved with an ornate design of vines and small flowers.

A beautiful antique mirror with a dark walnut frame hung over the fireplace in the room to the right. She could picture her bedroom in there. Tori mentally placed her bed in the corner and a chaise next to the fireplace.

There was a double window that offered a view to the front of the property and a window on the other side, giving her a view of the back of the farm.

The cabin had superb trim work and also had recessed lighting, a feature Tori loved. The main living area had cedar bookshelves. Tori was glad the cabin was all on one floor because she hated climbing stairs. The current homeowners had built a new addition to the cabin which held a sitting room and a brand new kitchen with stainless steel appliances and black granite countertops. This place was a steal at $160k.

"I'm interested, but I need a PDF sent to my email with a house inspection. I'll offer $145k in cash, if the house is sound. What about the barn? May I see it?" Tori looked at the Realtor's eyes and knew he was salivating for a sale.

"The barn was renovated for horses. It has electricity, running water, and a bathroom. Do you ride?" Andy smiled at Tori.

The barn sealed the deal. The opening in the back of the barn overlooked a hollow and a pond. She could hire a contractor to turn the barn into her studio if the seller took her offer. "Well, my offer stands, Andy."

"Miss Frost, I'll present your offer to the homeowners, but I think you may have a deal."

***

Two weeks later, Tori had moved all of her belongings into the cabin. She also adopted a full-grown black Labrador she named Jett because her mom had been a huge fan of Joan Jett. Tori had adopted Jett to stave off her loneliness because she missed her parents so much. They had died nearly five years ago in a massive flood that had hit Nashville. Terry and Sarah were in their car on the interstate when the flash flood had swept them away into a steep ravine. Tori still couldn't believe they were gone. Her parents had left her well-off, but that was her rainy-day money. It was her insurance policy in case her art didn't work out.

Tori's cell rang, startling her. She wiped the tears from her eyes as she looked at her reflection in the antique mirror. "Yello. Tori Frost, speaking."

Max, who was also a good friend, was on the line. He said excitedly, "Tori, darling, your smaller pieces have sold for a small fortune. You have a gift, girl, and now New York has noticed. The Columbus Art Gallery wants you to do a show. This could be it, beloved." It was nice to have Max looking out for her.

"Maxey, darling, I just moved. It'll be at least two months before my studio is ready. I've set up a makeshift studio in my breezeway. Please see if they will book me for next summer, maybe late July." Tori walked over and sat down on the plush chaise which reminded her of a favorite childhood teddy bear. It was dark brown and very soft. "And hey, when are you coming to see my new place?"

Max sighed and then replied, "Now, don't get your panties in a twist. I'm planning to drive out Halloween and spend the night. We'll tell ghost stories and drink merlot—and lots of it."

"I can't wait to see you. You know I love you more than my liver." She giggled and then glanced up at the antique mirror hanging over the fireplace in her bedroom. Tori rubbed her eyes and blinked several times.

A man was staring down at her from the other side of the mirror.

Jett nudged her hand and she briefly looked down at her dog. When she looked back up at the mirror, the man was gone.

"Tori, Tori, are you still there? I'm talking to you. Hello?"

"Maxey? Do you believe in ghosts?" Tori's tongue was so dry it stuck to the roof of her mouth and the room became quite chilly. She grabbed the quilt off the back of the chaise and draped it around her shoulders.

Tori heard the panic in Max's voice. "What the hell is going on, Tori? You're scaring the crap out of me."

Tori shivered as she stared at the mirror. "I guess I'm going batshit crazy because I swear a well-built, handsome man was just looking at me from the other side of my mirror. I need a dirty martini, extra dirty."

"Handsome man? Oh now, that's right down my alley, ghost or not. Share please. What did he look like?"

Tori walked over to the mantle to get a better look at the mirror. Specks of silver were missing from the glass, but it only added to the mirror's charm. "He's gone. That's so weird. I've had a glimpse of a shadow once or twice walking by the mirror in my bedroom, but this time a man was staring at me. He looked to be around my age with silky, golden hair, and I think his eyes were hazel, maybe a light brown. No idea how tall, but my god, Maxey, he had a red and black checkered flannel on like the Brawny guy. *Gorgeous.* I definitely need a man; it's been way too long and now, apparently, I'm seeing things."

Tori heard a deep laugh resonating from within the looking glass. "Holy shit, Max, now I'm hearing things. I think I just heard him laugh. Maxey, come out tonight, *please.* I need a drink." Tori turned and swiftly made her way into the kitchen, laid down her phone and clicked on the speaker. She grabbed her martini shaker from the freezer and mixed a rather strong drink. "Do you think I'm losing my mind out here in the sticks?"

"No, but I do think you're overworked and very tired from the move. Sometimes our minds can play tricks on us. Honey, I wish I could come out tonight, but I can't. I have plans to go to Dirk's soiree. I love you, darling, but I can't miss it. Besides, I work for other artists, not just you. *Although*, you are my favorite chicken."

Tori took a sip of her cocktail, picked up her phone and walked back into her bedroom. "And you're my Tennessee lamb. It was probably my imagination playing tricks on me anyway, with this cabin being so old and all."

Max said, "Got to go, precious. Ta-ta, pookie!"

"Have fun tonight, Maxey." Tori pushed the end button on her cell and laid her phone on the table next to the chaise. She looked up at the mirror. Did she really see and hear a man in her antique mirror? Or had she finally snapped?

After her second martini, Tori relaxed and felt a pretty good buzz coming on. Jett climbed onto the chaise with her and she began rubbing his ears. "You are no guard dog." She took another sip, and then she heard laughter again.

Tori knew she should be scared out of her wits, but she was intoxicated enough to be brave. Tori bellowed out into the room, "Okay, Mr. Hottie, or whomever the hell you are. I hear you and I've seen you." She shook her fist at the mirror. "Show yourself, because I've paid too much money on this place to pack it in and leave." Tori didn't really expect a reply. She had long been used to talking to herself.

The beautiful man appeared back in the mirror and looked down at her with a smirk. *Aw, hell.* A tingling sensation shot down her spine and she smiled in spite of herself. The ghost was effing hot and she wondered what it would be like to touch those incredibly sexy lips. Hell, forget just touching—she wanted to kiss them.

Tori watched as the specter placed his hand on the mirror and a room materialized behind him. The room had a rustic farmhouse kind of charm, with a plain kitchen table and four chairs. Behind the table, in the corner, she could see a beautifully carved headboard with several brightly patterned quilts thrown across the bed. The lighted gas lanterns cast the room with a soft, golden glow. But it was the man who took Tori's full attention. He was ruggedly handsome, with broad shoulders and narrow hips.

The ghost's voice was deep. "You really like to hear yourself yap, don't you?" The man continued to peer down at her with a smile curving his lips.

Tori's mouth dropped open for about two seconds, and then she drained the rest of her martini. "Jesus, Mary and Joseph, are you a ghost?"

"Ma'am, I mean no disrespect, but it's probably not a good idea to use the Lord's name like that, especially when you have been partaking." He chuckled and Tori melted against Jett.

Why couldn't he be a real man and not some apparition? That's just not fair. And he talked funny—like who would say "partaking" and "ma'am."

"Who are you and why are you in my mirror?" Jett hopped down from the chaise and ran out into the kitchen and through the doggie door to the backyard.

The mirror man laughed and said, "It's my mirror, not yours."

Tori should have been running out her front door, screaming, but she was drawn to the mirror as the man continued to stare at her so intensely. She walked up to the mirror and reached up to place her hand on the looking glass. The mirror became fluid and the man's hand reached through it to hold Tori's hand. Instantly, she was pulled into the other side—into a different world. Tori stood right in front of the mirror man and gulped.

"No, I'm not a ghost. I'm cursed." His eyes locked onto hers and she inhaled his scent—cloves and cinnamon.

Tori felt an incredible sexual attraction to this man. She reached up and touched the side of his face. "You're real?" she said in wide-eyed shock.

The cursed man stood only inches from her, so close she could feel the warmth of his breath. "You are magnificent," he said.

Whoa Nelly! Butterflies shot from her belly to her nether regions. "Okay, I know I'm probably having a hallucination brought on from being tired, and very strong vodka. I'm going to wake up any minute and you're going to disappear. Do you have a name or are you nameless until your curse is lifted?"

He laughed—a wonderful, hearty laugh—and replied, "My name is Jonathan Rogers." Jonathan placed a kiss on the back of Tori's hand and looked up at her. His expression darkened and then he said, "Victoria, I have cursed you now, too."

Tori stumbled backward and tripped over a stool, falling hard on the wooden floor. Jonathan bent down to help her up and she jerked away from him. "What the hell are you talking about? Why would I be cursed?"

Jonathan motioned toward the table and chairs and said, "Please, sit down." He gazed into Tori's eyes with a look that struck a familiar chord with her; it was loneliness.

"I would like to tell you my life story and how I ended up in this cursed mirror," Jonathan said. Tori blinked a couple of times and then nodded.

"In 1915, my life was just beginning. I owned a thousand-acre farm. I had a hundred head of cattle, and had just built this cabin. I was in love with a woman who loved me back and we were to be married." Jonathan walked over to the window and stared outside. "Her name was Mae Morgan and her father was the president of the local bank. He had arranged for his only daughter to marry one of his business partners, and I got in the way."

Tori interrupted him and asked, "Where was Mae's mother?"

Jonathan returned to sit at the table with Tori. "Mae's mother died when she was very young. Mae only had her father and me."

Jonathan's voice sounded rough around the edges. "Mae stood up to her father, and refused to marry his business partner, Dale Rogers. Dale apparently had invested heavily in future business development projects with Mr. Morgan. Mae's father was using her as collateral. Mr. Morgan told Mae he'd rather see her dead than married to me. Mr. Morgan telephoned Dale after an argument with Mae and arranged for Dale and Mae to be married the next day. That's when Mae decided to run away, to me."

Jonathan looked down at his hands, where they were resting on the table, and then he looked back up at Tori. "Mae left home with only her mother's mirror, the one that's now hanging over the mantle, and the clothes on her back." He walked to the mantle and ran his fingers along the wooden frame. "Mae knocked on my door right before midnight, terribly shaken and scared for her life." Jonathan walked over into the little kitchen and grabbed a dipper out of a pail and took a drink of water. He said, "Would you like some water?"

With an uplifted brow, Tori said, "Any chance you have anything stronger?"

Jonathan opened a cupboard and pulled out a jug like she had only seen in reruns of *The Beverly Hillbillies*, and poured her a cup. Tori took it and greedily drank. It was moonshine and it was strong. Tori coughed several times, but felt more at ease once the alcohol hit her bloodstream.

"Okay, you can continue now," Tori said. "No one's ever going to believe me anyway." She wasn't convinced Jonathan or his story was real. She was probably passed out on her bedroom floor and would wake up in the morning with a hell of a hangover.

Jonathan poured himself a cup of the moonshine and sat back down at the table. He took a small sip and said, "Mae had left her father a note saying she was marrying me. I found out later he jumped into his 1914 Chevrolet Baby Grand and drove to the witches' coven located at the outskirts of town and paid for a curse. He'd rather his daughter be dead than disgraced in front of his inner social circle."

Jonathan didn't talk for several minutes. Tori sensed he was angry and kept her mouth shut. He began to pace back and forth across the room. "My neighbor and good friend was a pastor. I had no intention of disgracing Mae by allowing her to spend the night with me. We went to his house and he married us. By the time we returned to the cabin, dawn was approaching. I swept her in my arms and carried her over the threshold. I laid her down on our bed and made love to my wife."

Jonathan stared into the mirror and then turned back to face Tori. "I didn't realize Jasmine, the youngest of the witches, was watching us from outside the window. She could see us from the reflection of this mirror, which gave her the idea for the incantation."

Jonathan eyes glazed over as he began to recite the curse. "As the happy couple consummates their wedding bed, the wife will die in ecstasy, and her groom will live a mirrored destiny, until a new love opens a thread and pulls him back to reality."

Jonathan sat down in the rocking chair next to the fireplace. "After we made love, I watched helplessly as Mae died in my arms. Then the witch burst through my door. Jasmine told me I would meet a new love, and that love would set me free of the mirrored life. She said Mae's father had paid for the curse that took Mae's life and left me cursed to live here. Jasmine stood staring at me and I could feel her desire and it scared me. I thought she was going to kiss me, when she spun around instead, and disappeared right in front of my eyes."

With sadness, Jonathan said, "I'm so sorry, Victoria. I watched you move into my cabin and was so drawn to you. I've never wanted to reveal myself to anyone before you. You are the one to set me free. But as much as I was drawn to you, I still knew better. If you touched the mirror and then I touched your hand, you would cross over to me."

Tori shook her head in disbelief as the realization hit her like a ton of bricks—she was his ticket out. She jumped up and shouted, "What? This can't be real! I don't believe this! I can't be stuck here. I have a life, a wonderful career that's really taking off. I just adopted

Jett." She ran her fingers through her ebony hair as she paced about the room. "Okay, there has to be a way to break the curse. Surely there's a way."

Jonathan held her gaze and without wavering said, "There's a way. We have to fall in love by this All Hallows' Eve to break the curse and we'll be set free. It's only two weeks away. The Pleiades star cluster, also known as the Seven Sisters, will almost be overhead on midnight of All Hallows' Eve. The star cluster signals not only the night of the dead, but offers us a window in time to cross back through the mirror, which will break the curse. If we don't fall in love, it will be another year before the window opens again."

Tori screamed in frustration and stormed over and smacked him hard across his face. She ran out the front door and onto the porch. The brisk air cut her to the bone and she started to shiver. The trees were emblazoned with the colors of fall as she looked around the property—which was owned by both her and Jonathan, although a hundred years apart. Tori pondered the impossible situation: she had two weeks to fall in love with a complete stranger.

Tori still couldn't believe she was really here in 1915 with a man who had pulled her across time to break him free from a hundred-year-old curse. Surely, she would wake up from this nightmare. "What am I going to do now?" she muttered to herself.

Jonathan joined her on the porch and set down a pair of boots, and then wrapped a quilt around her shoulders. She turned to face him and he pulled her into his arms. He brushed his lips softly across her cheek and up to her ear, and then whispered, "I should be sorry I pulled you across time, but I'm not." Jonathan crushed

her with a kiss that would have knocked her socks off—
had she been wearing any.

Victoria broke from his kiss and pushed him away.
"Thanks for the boots." She slipped her feet inside the
boots and walked down the steps. "I have to clear my
head." She continued walking around the outside of the
cabin. In the backyard, beyond the white fence, she saw
an outhouse and a cellar. She walked down the steps of
the cellar and nearly fell out of the borrowed boots
because they were too big for her feet. "Victoria,
Victoria, you're not in Kansas anymore and these are
definitely not ruby slippers." Tori felt Jonathan walk up
behind her. Yes, she was attracted to Jonathan—but
would she fall in love with him? And within two weeks,
no less. Tori turned and gazed into his eyes. He really was
beautiful.

Jonathan placed his hand on her shoulder. "Not
much changes on this side of the mirror, but on your
side, I have seen so many changes. Radio and television,
stereos and Xboxes. I've watched mankind evolve into a
self-indulgent society. It's not a bad thing. But, with all
the conveniences of your generation, people have
forgotten the sacrifices of those who came before them."

Victoria replied, "I suppose we are very used to our
conveniences. Running water—I will never take it for
granted again." Tori shivered from the cold and he
wrapped his big, muscular arms around her. The warmth
from his body made her instantly heat up. It felt nice to
be in a man's arms, if only briefly, but then she pushed
him away.

Tori felt really confused and didn't understand
what was happening to her. She didn't want her sexual
attraction to Jonathan to cloud her already-buzzed brain.

Tori walked out of the cellar. "Jonathan, I need some time alone. I'm going for a walk."

Jonathan stepped out of her way. "Follow this tractor trail behind the cabin. The trail circles back to the barn. I'll be here if you need me, just holler."

"I will," Victoria said. She knew the way because it was her property, too.

Tori walked along the trail behind the cabin. She came across a few squirrels and rabbits, and off to the left she saw a small pond where a deer was taking a drink of water. The cabin disappeared behind her as she turned onto a bend in the trail.

Suddenly, out of nowhere, a woman appeared on a log stump. She looked to be Tori's age, with piercing green eyes that reminded Tori of a cat's. The woman was exotically beautiful, with her smooth olive skin and inky black hair. The woman stood and approached Tori. She said, "Hello, Victoria. I'm Jasmine, the witch who cursed Jonathan."

Tori turned to run, but the witch grabbed her wrist and shouted, "Be still." Tori was unable to move; the witch had paralyzed her.

This day just keeps getting better and better, Tori thought.

"Don't be afraid, child. If I wanted to harm you, I would have." The witch released her and walked slowly around Victoria. "Now, I see my Jonathan has selected his new mate. Are you worthy?" The witch waved her hand. "Don't answer that. I've been watching you since you came onto this property. You're alone, so is Jonathan. It's only natural for him to be attracted to you."

Tori tried to speak, but she couldn't open her mouth. The witch walked over to stand within inches of her, searching out every line and crevice of Tori's face.

"You wish to speak?" She touched Tori's lips.

Tori opened her mouth and then closed it. What if she said something that pissed the witch off and she turned her into a toad? But curiosity got the best of her and Tori said, "Can't you reverse the curse? You obviously seem to care something for Jonathan if you've been watching him for a hundred years."

The witch shouted, "Be silent! You know nothing of this matter. You're simply a means to an end." Jasmine began to study Tori and trailed her long, slender fingers over Tori's skin, which made her flesh crawl. The witch said wickedly, "Mae was never good enough for Jonathan and you aren't either. My coven has strict rules on intervening on behalf of humans, and especially regarding reversing curses. I am forbidden, even if I wanted to help Jonathan. If I had only seen Jonathan before I cast the spell, I would have spared him. I would have made him mine. But you, my dear, you only have to get him to fall in love with you. And then once he returns to the real world, you may go back to your own life."

Tori didn't believe for one minute the witch would allow her to live. Tori could feel the evil surrounding the witch. She had killed Mae and god knows who else in the last hundred years. Tori was in a lose-lose situation.

"I thought the curse said we had to fall in love with each other by All Hallows' Eve or we would be cursed to spend another year here together." Tori's eyes widened and she said, "That's it, you want me to fall in love with him now, before Halloween because if I don't, he will live with me for a year. A lot can happen in a year."

Jasmine seemed to glow a bluish-gray color. Tori knew instantly she had overstepped her boundaries.

"You're unlike Mae," the witch said. "Very intelligent, too smart for your own good. Yes, the love must be reciprocated, but once you're back in your own time, I will place a spell on Jonathan breaking him free of your love. Then, he will be mine."

Tori was afraid of the witch, but also felt pity for her. True love held its own magic and could not be paved with a curse. Tori had no idea if she would fall in love with Jonathan, but she didn't want him to fall into the witch's hands, either.

"Why can't you cast a spell on him now? You *are* in love with him, aren't you?"

"Silence!" Jasmine pointed her finger in Tori's face and without thinking Tori grabbed it. The witch jerked her hand away and tossed Tori several feet into the air. Then the witch turned Tori upside down and left her dangling there. For the first time in Tori's life, she felt a paralyzing fear. Tori could feel the witch's desire to kill her.

Jonathan ran up behind the witch and yelled, "Jasmine, don't hurt her." Jasmine wheeled on him, hissed, and then vanished.

Jonathan dashed underneath Victoria to protect her from crashing to the ground. Tori fell on top of Jonathan and then threw her arms around his neck, and lost it. She shook uncontrollably as she tried to tell Jonathan what had happened with the witch.

Tori pulled slightly away from Jonathan and said, "She wants me dead. I could feel it. Jasmine wants to kill me. She has a seriously unhealthy attachment to you and wants you for herself. I don't think she has any intention of allowing me to live, once she gets what she wants."

"Victoria, she's a murderer and I hate her. I'll find a way to protect you. I will not lose you like I lost Mae." He wrapped his arms around Tori, pulling her against his chest, and rocked her back and forth.

Jonathan had saved her, but for how long? She broke from his embrace and searched his eyes. "How can you protect me from her? How? She's a friggin' witch!"

Jonathan caressed the side of her face with his hand and said, "I don't have many books, but I do have one about Cherokee folklore, legends and myths. There's a chapter on protection against evil. That's why I made this." He showed her the necklace around his neck. "It's a talisman to protect me from the witch and other evil spirits. I will make one for you, too."

**

The next day, Tori tried to acclimate to living in the early 20th Century. Tori had lost her temper several times learning how to draw water from the well and how to cook on a potbellied stove. Jonathan was a kind, gentle and very patient teacher. Living in this altered state of reality was hard, but Tori felt a sense of accomplishment when she mastered a task, like washing clothes on the rudimentary machine on the back porch.

Tori and Jonathan sat at the kitchen table talking after supper. Jonathan excitedly talked about the time he had heard Teddy Roosevelt speak. Jonathan moved his hands all about while talking. "Teddy Roosevelt was larger than life," he said. "My father and I heard him speak when he was McKinley's running mate in the election of 1900."

Tori walked over to the fireplace and turned her back to the fire to feel its warmth. "The only place I've ever seen our president is on TV. Jonathan, we're from two way different time periods, but I'm glad we're getting to know each other."

Jonathan walked over to join her and brushed the back of his fingers down her cheek and reached over and gently kissed her. "I watched you for two weeks when you moved into the cabin and this is what I have learned about you. You love your dog. You talk to your plants like they're babies. The night you brought your easel into your bedroom and began to paint on your canvas was pure magic. You should have seen the expression on your face. You love your art. I want you to look at me like that."

Jonathan trailed his fingers down to the hollow spot at the base of her neck and leaned over and kissed her there. "You're so stunningly beautiful and you have the most insane sense of humor when you're talking on the phone with your friend, Max." He kissed her this time on her lips and she melted against him.

When she broke from his kiss, Tori eyes brightened and her cheeks were flushed pink. "I think I'm a little jealous of Mae. It's gonna be kind of hard to compete with the memory of a dead woman." *Oh shit.* The stare he just gave her sent chills up her arm. Why did she have to say "dead woman"?

Jonathan's eyes darkened and he stepped away from Tori. "Don't ever speak of Mae. Not ever." He grabbed his coat and stalked out of the cabin.

Tori fell back on the bed and threw her arm across her eyes. "I'm so screwed. How in the hell did this happen to me? I'm falling for someone who is so obviously still hung up on his dead wife." Tori heard Jett barking and she jumped out of bed and ran to the mirror. Jett was looking at her from the other side. He barked and wagged his tail.

"Jett, can you hear me, boy? Can you see me? I miss you, sweetie." Jett had probably been fending for himself, going in and out of the doggie door to relieve himself and forage for food. Jett was barking like crazy when Tori heard Max come in her front door.

"Victoria! *Tori*, are you here? I've called your cell numerous times and it went straight to voice mail so I got worried. Where are you, chicken?" He walked into her bedroom and looked up into the mirror and saw her on the other side.

Tori waved weakly. "Hi, my Tennessee lamb. You know the ghost, well he ain't a ghost. He's cursed. I foolishly touched the mirror and he grabbed ahold of my hand, and the next thing I knew I crossed over into one of those PBS 1900 House episodes."

Max stood frozen, with his mouth wide open for a couple of seconds, but then walked over to touch the mirror.

Tori screamed, "Don't, Maxey! The mirror could suck you in, too."

Max jumped back and covered his mouth. "Well, kiss my grits," he said. "This is... this is... so *insane*. Can't I try and grab you out of there? Good lord, how did the curse happen?" Max placed one hand on his hip.

Oh, she loved Max Dupres. "This is the down and dirty. The mirror man's name is Jonathan and he was in love with a woman named Mae. His intended's deranged father paid a witch to curse them. Mae ran away to Brawny and they were married. The curse kicked in when they made love, killing Mae and spinning Brawny into this mirrored life. Jonathan has to fall in love again to break the curse. That's where I come in. And I met the witch who cast the curse, Jasmine. She wants me dead." Tori placed her hand on the mirror as the tears began to stream down her face.

"Chicken, please don't cry. We'll figure something out. I have friends in many circles. I just bet I can find something to nullify the curse. Where's Brawny now and what's he like?" Max placed his hand on the mantle.

Tori cried and then laughed. "Jonathan is wonderful and kind. I haphazardly referred to his wife as a dead woman and he got pissed off and stalked out of the cabin." Then, she started to giggle at how ridiculous the whole thing sounded.

Max smiled and wagged his index finger at her. "My god, Tori, you really like this man."

Tori's leveled her eyes at Max. "I do not! He... he is... aw, hell, he's in love with his dead wife. How am I supposed to compete with a memory? Oh, there's one more problem with the curse. Jonathan has to fall in love with me by this Halloween and I have to love him back or I'll be stuck in here for at least another year and you can kiss the New York show good-bye. If we do fall in love with each other, then Jonathan and I can escape the mirror and I might have a new date to the Frist Christmas Gala."

Max rubbed his shiny bald head. "I've got to get you out of there! I wonder if they have anything in the local library about the witch coven. Obviously, since you met the witch, the coven must still exist. Maybe some locals would know how to help us expedite you out of the mirror. You're living in 1915?" He chuckled.

Tori nodded and stepped back so Max could look around Jonathan's room. "No running water, no electricity, no phone and no bathroom! I had to use an outhouse for a toilet." Max started laughing. "Stop it, Max, it's not funny. Would you take care of Jett for me? I've been so worried about him."

Max turned and saw Jett sitting beside him. "Okay, I will take care of Jett. But, I'm not going anywhere until I meet Brawny."

Jonathan walked back inside the cabin and over to Tori, and then he looked at Max. "Who is Brawny?"

Max gave him a once-over and lifted an eyebrow. "You are a doll."

Tori laughed and then made the introductions, and told Jonathan about Max going to search out the locals to see if anyone could help them.

With a look of concern, Jonathan said, "I wouldn't advise it. The witches would kill you or us if they feel threatened in any way."

Max eyes widened. "Duly noted. I will steer clear of the witch coven and the locals. I have to go out of town with another artist, but I'll be back on Halloween. I'll call my friend who practices witchcraft. He may know something of the curse. I'll take Jett with me. Jonathan, take care of my girl." Max blew Tori a kiss and said, "I love you, pookie."

"I love you, Max. Be careful." Tori watched Max and Jett walk out into the foyer and heard the front door shut.

Jonathan turned Tori to face him. "I'm sorry I lost my temper. You may have misunderstood why I got mad. I've made some peace with Mae's death, but I'll always love her and I still feel responsible for her death. Victoria, you don't have to compete with anyone, much less the memory of Mae. You just have to decide whether you can love me or not. I'm falling in love with you and it is much more intense than the first time, with Mae." Jonathan grabbed her by the nape of her neck and covered her with kisses. Desire fisted sharply at the base of her spine as she pressed against the length of Jonathan.

Jonathan whispered murmurings of love, in between his kisses, and she desperately wanted to believe him. For the moment, Tori allowed herself to be caught in a whirlwind of emotion and she lost herself in his embrace.

***

Over the next couple of weeks, Tori helped Jonathan pick the remaining vegetables from his garden and the apples from his orchard. He taught her how to can vegetables and make jam.

They raked the fall leaves around the small yard and Jonathan made a large pile of leaves for them to jump in, like they were kids. Jonathan loved to laugh and his laughter was contagious.

At bedtime, Jonathan made a pallet on the floor close to the bed where Tori slept. They would talk until one of them fell asleep. The nights Jonathan fell asleep first, Tori wondered what it would be like to spend the rest of her life with him. She would glance out the window and the moon seemed to smile at her, like they shared a cosmic secret. Tori knew the curse had brought her through the mirror, but it was love, making her want to stay. Yes, she admitted to herself, she was falling in love with Jonathan more and more every day.

Tori had mixed emotions the day All Hallows' Eve arrived. Part of her wanted to stay with Jonathan in his isolated 1915 world, and part of her longed for home. Jonathan took her fishing that morning at his pond and they carved a couple of pumpkins during the afternoon. As dusk turned into nightfall, Jonathan placed lit candles inside the jack-o'-lanterns.

Jonathan and Tori sat in front of the fireplace, talking after supper. Tori talked about the first time she watched the movie *Halloween* with Jamie Lee Curtis, and how the villain, Michael Myers, couldn't be killed.

Jonathan wrinkled his nose. "Why would you want to watch something so terrifying?"

Tori looked at him sheepishly. "As silly as this sounds, people in my time love watching scary movies."

With a raised brow, he said, "Isn't the world frightening enough?"

Tori reached over and held his hand. "The world is frightening and tonight scares me to death. I'm frightened I may die, but what scares me the most is the thought of losing you."

Jonathan smiled at her. "Come here and sit on my lap." Tori climbed onto his lap. He brushed her hair off one shoulder and she linked an arm around his neck. "Victoria, sweet, sweet, Victoria, I'll never regret our time together. If I die tonight, I'll die a happy man. I'm so in love with you."

Tori's face lit up with a dazzling smile. "And I'm in love with you, too. No matter what." She closed her eyes and kissed him.

"My, my, my—isn't this a witch's dream come true." Jasmine appeared behind them.

They jumped up from the rocker and Jonathan placed Tori behind him.

Jasmine said, "Look at the mirror, Jonathan. You and Tori have broken the curse and now all you have to do is place your hands on the mirror and you'll be free." Jasmine sneered as she paced about them. "What are you waiting for? Go!"

Tori turned around to find ripples rolling across the mirror, like waves on the ocean. Tori said a silent prayer of protection for her and Jonathan. The time had come to go.

Jonathan squared his shoulders and grabbed Tori's hands. "Do you trust me, Tori?"

Time seemed to stand still before she finally answered, "I trust you, Jonathan."

Jonathan quickly replied, "Then hold on tight." Jonathan scooped Victoria up in his arms and stepped up on the stool by the fireplace and catapulted them through the mirror. They fell through to the other side. Jonathan quickly picked up a fire iron and smashed the mirror before the witch could follow them.

Victoria ducked as fragments of the mirror sprayed across her bedroom. She reached down and picked up a jagged piece of glass and saw Jasmine pointing her finger at Tori. She dropped the piece on the floor and crushed it with the heel of her boot. "Jonathan, she's still in the mirror."

Jonathan didn't pick up the glass. He said, "Do you have a broom?"

"Yes." As Tori ran into her laundry room to get the broom, she heard the front door open. It was Max and Jett. Tori ran to Max. "Quick, Max, put Jett in the den and shut the door. The witch tried to follow us through the mirror, but Jonathan smashed it. There's glass everywhere and I don't want Jett to get hurt. The witch is still in there, in the shards of glass." Tori pointed to her bedroom.

Max quickly took Jett into the den and shut the door. Then he followed Tori into her bedroom. Max was carrying a huge leather-bound book and ran to the table beside the chaise and flipped it open. "A friend let me borrow this book. It is full of curses. I found this today. There are several curses in here regarding mirrors. But this one is eerily close to what you've been living in, Jonathan."

Jonathan picked up the book of curses and stifled a groan. With a frown, he tossed a glance to Max and then turned to Victoria. Jonathan said, "This is the curse Jasmine used on Mae and me."

Tori anxiously said, "Does it say anything about broken mirrors? That evil witch is still in there. She may know how to escape."

Jonathan said, "I'll start a fire and you sweep up the pieces. We'll throw the shards in the flames and then maybe the fire will burn her alive."

Tori began to sweep up the broken pieces as Jonathan started a fire and Max continued to read the book of curses. They looked at each other wide-eyed with alarm when Jasmine began to loudly chant from the broken pieces:

"Broken mirrors never clearer, cursed mirror bring me nearer, hear me now and make them quiver. Mirror, Mirror, hear my cry, die fools die, for I'm your killer."

Tori threw her broom down and screamed with fear. She yelled at Jasmine, "Stop! Stop!" and covered her ears.

Max picked up the broom and scooped up the pieces into the dust pan and yelled at Jasmine, "Shut up, Witch!"

Jonathan had the fire blazing until the room was so hot they were all sweating. He glanced over his shoulder and shouted at Max, "Hurry, throw the pieces in the fire now!"

As the shards of glass hit the flames, sparks flew out into Tori's bedroom. Tori and Max stomped out the embers with their boots. Suddenly, a shrill cry ripped through the room and they all watched as the glass melted and simply vanished away.

Max rubbed his head. Out of breath, he said, "Tori, do you have any whiskey?"

Tori ran out into her kitchen and opened the liquor cabinet. She grabbed a bottle of Gentlemen Jack and placed it on the tray from the kitchen counter and grabbed three shot glasses. Tori was visibly shaken when she returned to her bedroom and placed the tray on the table beside the chaise, nearly dropping it all on the floor before Max came to her aid. She poured them each a shot and drained hers quickly. Pale and still frightened, she said, "Is she gone? Is Jasmine gone?"

Jonathan walked over and picked up his shot and drank it. He wiped his mouth with the back of his hand and then said, "I think so. What time is it?"

Max reached inside his pocket and pulled out his iPhone. "It's 11:55, almost midnight and All Saints Day." Max grabbed his whiskey shot and drank it and then poured another. "Holy shit. If I hadn't seen it with my own eyes, I would have never believed what happened here."

Jonathan pulled Tori against him and slipped his arm around her waist and she leaned against his shoulder. Jonathan looked down at her and said, "Are you okay, Tori?"

Tori gave him a weak smile and said, "I am now. Is Jasmine really dead, Jonathan?" Tori looked back at the fire. Her blood still thundered through her veins and she recalled Michael Myers and shivered at the thought that Jasmine could still be out there.

Jonathan leaned down and kissed her, and then caressed the side of her face with his hand. "Yes, Jasmine is dead."

Max poured them all another round and then raised his glass. "Ding, freaking dong! The wicked witch is dead."

THE END

ABOUT KATE BARAY

Author of *The Covered Mirror*

Kate Baray writes urban & paranormal fantasy, frequently with a romantic twist. She writes and lives in Austin, Texas with her pack of pointers and a bloodhound. Kate has worked as an attorney, a manager, a tractor sales person, and a dog trainer, but writing is her passion. When she's not writing, she volunteers with a search and rescue team, sweeps up hairy dust bunnies, and watches British mysteries.

Website: www.katebaray.com
Newsletter: http://eepurl.com/WD6UD
Twitter: @KateBarayAuthor
Facebook: www.facebook.com/katebaray

An Excerpt from

SPIRELLI PARANORMAL INVESTIGATIONS: EPISODE 1

By Kate Baray

Chapter 1

Jack fiddled with the inner workings of his ancient cash register. He needed a newer machine to better track sales, because— shocker—The Junk Shop had a few sales to track. Who knew boxes of garage sale rejects would be so popular? The store hours were erratic, and the stock ranged from recycled trash to bizarre trinkets, yet the store still received stellar online consumer reviews. It didn't have a website. So how did the yuppies, hipsters—whoever the hell was writing the damn reviews—find it?

"You know, that car outside looks like it needs a little work. I might know a guy, if you're interested."

Five foot and a lot, the woman attached to the voice would be hard to miss, with her fiery red hair and startlingly bright green eyes. Jack left his barstool perch behind the counter and had a long look at her. He'd missed her entering the store, and her voice had startled him. Quite a task, considering he had the store warded like mad. And he was hardly an unobservant guy.

"How can I help you?" Jack worked to produce a convincingly relaxed tone.

Face expressionless, the redhead said, "I'm here to apply for the position."

"We're not hiring at the moment." When she didn't reply and she also didn't leave, he added, "Look around. We're a small shop, but maybe something will catch your eye."

Sure, The Junk Shop was a retail location, but it had begun primarily as a front for Jack's work with the magic-using community. A discreet physical location was a bonus when meeting with clients who wanted to stay under the radar. He looked around the small store. For a front, it was becoming increasingly and uncomfortably popular.

She looked around. "Uh-huh. I'm not here for…bric-a-brac. I'm sure you've got a position open. My sources are excellent."

Jack hadn't posted the position. Where would he? He could just imagine how that ad would read. *Wanted: paranormal investigator's assistant. Complete discretion and some ass-kicking required. Part-time help in The Junk Shop mandatory. A high tolerance for the unexplainable preferred.* No.

And Jack had only mentioned to a select few that he was looking to hire: his highest-ranking Inter-Pack Policing Cooperative contact, Harrington; the Texas Pack leader, John Braxton; and IPPC's temporary chief of security for the Prague library, Ewan Campbell.

"Who's your reference?"

"My stealth entry into the store wasn't reference enough?" She gave him a toothy smile.

That smile made him incredibly uncomfortable. Green eyes, creepy feeling—alarm bells were ringing.

Fuck. His stealthy, green-eyed Amazon was a dragon. He'd bet cash on it. He stared back without answering.

She shrugged. "Lachlan McClellan, but that might not be entirely to my benefit when you check my references."

"Head of the McClellan clan?"

The guy led a powerful clan of dragons, but he was also a dick with a crap sense of humor. And Jack didn't see him being particularly enlightened about female employees. Although he was surprised Ewan had mentioned Jack's staffing needs to his clan leader.

She hesitated before responding. "We're from the same clan."

Fuck yeah. Dragon. He knew it. "You want the job?"

She raised an eyebrow. "I'm here, having this conversation with you."

Her non-answers were annoying as hell. More importantly, he didn't see it becoming less annoying with time and proximity.

"Pass." Jack turned back to the register.

"Wait. Yes, I would like the job." She continued to speak to his back. "Please. I would very much like this job."

Slowly Jack turned around. "Then tell me why I should hire you? Besides your stealth entry into a warded store. That only tells me you're a thief."

A brief flicker of fiery green flashed in her eyes, but quickly dimmed. "I'm unemployed and unable to return to my previous employer, which makes me highly motivated to be successful here. Also, I understand you're looking for muscle. My combat skills are excellent." She blinked. "I can demonstrate."

She gave him another smile with just a shade too many teeth.

"No thanks. A dragon kicking my very human ass isn't much of a demonstration. Besides, I'd hate for us to break my bric-a-brac." Jack sat down behind the counter and picked up a pen. Having a dragon would be a huge tactical advantage in most fights, regardless of technical competence.

"Talk to Lachlan. Whatever else he might say, he'll tell you I'm honest and hardworking." She placed a slight emphasis on "honest." She swallowed, the first sign of nervousness she'd displayed since walking into his store. "Please."

Apparently he'd hit a nerve when he'd compared her to a thief. A highly motivated, well-connected dragon employee—he'd be an idiot to walk away just because she wasn't exactly right. Especially since he didn't know what "exactly right" was. What type of person wouldn't drive him nuts with continuous contact? The shelf life of most of his relationships, regardless of the type, was pretty short.

"What's your name?"

"Marin." She didn't offer her hand.

Jack knew the right answer, yet still he hesitated. Damn. He had a job coming up day after tomorrow that could use some dragon muscle.

"All right, Marin. Come back tomorrow at ten. If your reference comes through, we'll discuss employment terms." He narrowed his eyes. "I don't pay well."

She ducked her chin once in acknowledgment and headed out the door. This time, Jack saw her pass through the ward, and a shower of green sparks, visible only to him, fell in her wake. He felt a corresponding pinch from the ring he wore on his right hand. No way he'd missed the ward triggering when she'd first entered the store. If this whole thing worked out and she joined Spirelli Paranormal Investigations, that was one of his first questions.

Jack picked up his cell and scrolled through his contacts, looking for Ewan's number. Jack was pretty sure Ewan would put him in touch with Lachlan. After a quick mental calculation, adding seven hours to account for Prague time, Jack decided it wasn't too late and dialed Ewan's number.

Ewan answered on the first ring. "Jack. What's up?"

"Hey, Ewan. Any chance you could put me in touch with Lachlan? I had someone come by the shop asking about that assistant's job. Remember, I told you I was looking for someone? Lachlan came up as a reference."

"Sure." Background noise filtered in. "Heads up—you're on speaker."

"Thanks, man. You might actually know her; she's from your clan. A tall redhead named Marin?"

The background noise abruptly disappeared. Ewan must have turned the speaker function off and picked up his phone. "Yeah." The word came out so short, it almost sounded like a grunt.

Something about Marin had drastically changed the tone of their conversation. Jack contemplated for a split second whether to ask. He closed his eyes. Had he lost his mind?

After a few seconds of silence, Ewan said, "Marin is my daughter."

Jack sat on his favorite barstool, the one positioned in front of the shop's register. Careful to make his tone as neutral as possible, he said, "I didn't know that."

"Clearly."

Jack didn't get it. Ewan seemed pissed, but the guy hadn't said a word about not hiring his kid. Since Jack wasn't eager to get singed or mutilated due to an unfortunate miscommunication, clarification was the wisest course. "So, are you telling me you don't want me to hire her?"

"Not at all."

Jesus. Really? Jack rolled his shoulders. "Are you telling me you want me to hire her?"

"What did you want to know?" Ewan's voice had lost some of its edge.

"Uh, okay." Jack figured Ewan had enough patience for about two questions, so he erred on the side of caution and limited himself to one. "Would you recommend Marin for the job?"

"Yes. We done?"

Good enough.

"Yeah. Thanks again." As he pocketed his phone, he caught a flash of movement out of the corner of his eye.

Staring at the now empty shop floor, he said, "I know you're there, little guy. You better be glad I know what rat poison does." He couldn't commit to chemical warfare—even in the pursuit of pest control. It was a weird quirk. Whatever. People who used rat poison must not know what that shit did to the insides of an animal. He snorted. Or they just didn't like living with rats. "Fuzzball, you're damn lucky I don't actually live in this pit."

Jack shook his head. He really needed to stop talking to the rats. It probably made them feel welcome. But he couldn't resist one last warning. "You better not touch the coffee, Fuzzface."

Chapter 2

Jack's ring tightened on his finger, interrupting his morning coffee ritual. He ignored the jingle of the front door bells and the flash of green light in his peripheral vision.

"You're early." Jack didn't raise his voice. He figured dragons had good hearing.

A few seconds later, Marin joined him in his office at the back of the store. "Nice bells."

Overkill maybe, but after Marin had surprised him yesterday they'd seemed like a good addition. "They were sitting around the store. That happens a lot, actually. I need something, have a look around, and there it is."

"Really?" She raised an eyebrow and tilted her head.

"What? It's a junk shop. That's not shocking. It's not like I keep great records on my stock. I buy most of this crap by the box." He opened the small fridge under the coffee station and pulled out milk.

"Hmm." She sat down in one of his client chairs. "And, by the way, I'm only five minutes early."

"The front door was locked." Jack tried to be pissed that she'd picked his front door lock, but he couldn't quite work up to it.

Marin stared back at him without comment.

"And I haven't had my coffee."

She glanced at the half-empty pot of coffee.

"I've only had one cup of coffee. And quit being such a smartass." When she didn't apologize—as if he thought she would—he asked, "Would you like a cup?"

"Yes, thank you."

He handed her a cup of black coffee. If she wanted milk or sugar, she was on her own. Once he'd sat down behind his desk, he said, "Minimum wage. Forty hours a week, no overtime, no benefits. You work in the shop or on cases, as I decide."

"Minimum wage?" She looked amused, rather than worried.

If she wasn't working for the cash, then why? He mentally thumped himself. Didn't matter and he didn't care. If it became relevant, then he'd worry about it.

"You came to me," Jack reminded her.

"Yes." She wrapped her hands around her coffee mug. Closely trimmed nails, no polish—practical.

He waited. He could use her. Needed her, really. But he wasn't about to start this relationship from a position of weakness.

Marin gave him an odd look he couldn't interpret, then said, "If that was an employment offer, I accept."

ABOUT STEVE STATHAM

Author of *On Wings of Steel*

Steve Statham began his writing career in the car magazine world, pounding out articles about cars with too much horsepower. He was the editor of a classic car magazine for many years and has had twelve non-fiction books on automotive subjects published. But his first love has always been science-fiction and fantasy and he now devotes most of his time to creating tales of far-flung adventure. Steve is the author of The Connor Rix Chronicles, SF thrillers that explore the secret world of bio-engineered superhumans. The series begins with *Rules of Force.* His contemporary fantasy novel *Follow the Chupacabra* brings the vivid legends of the American Southwest to life as the heroes explore endless pathways in a multiverse of alternate worlds. When not dreaming up strange futures, Steve tries to live a normal life in the Texas Hill Country with his wife, daughter and golden retriever.

Website: www.stevestatham.com
Newsletter: http://eepurl.com/YU5lH
Facebook: www.facebook.com/stevestathambooks

An Excerpt from

FOLLOW THE CHUPACABRA

By Steve Statham

Their heads broke above the waves. They gasped for air, kicking and thrashing to rise as far as they could above the surface of the water. They emerged into a trough, surrounded by walls of water, but large swells soon lifted them high.

There was no land in sight.

Galene searched frantically for Storm. She spied the dog about twenty feet away, paddling steadily toward her. She swam over and let the animal crawl partly onto her shoulders. Storm licked her ear, but the animal's claws dug painfully into her skin.

"Sorry, girl," she said. "But it looks like we've got a little further to go."

She saw Ray further behind her, swimming stiffly, eyes glassy.

"Ray! Are you okay?"

He nodded numbly.

Galene closed her eyes and whispered into the water. *Thank you, Great Lady.* She felt her own mark, the "touch" from a Foundation, as Ray and the chupacabras had described it, as a cool embrace around her ankle.

She rode another swell as it carried her up. The sun broke from behind scattered clouds, lighting the waves of an ocean that spread out in all directions, endless.

Galene had always been afraid this might happen one day, following a water path that ended up in an ocean. She had safely traversed many such underwater trails between worlds, but remembered from history classes in school that, in earlier geologic ages, the American Southwest had been covered by a shallow sea. In a world where infinite possibilities crowded in and overlapped, she always suspected that there could be an Earth where that never changed, and the Texas she knew would be no more than a seabed.

She swam toward Ray, kicking slowly and deliberately so Storm could ride on her back for a while longer.

"Hang in there, Ray. The path took us here, but we'll find another and get back to dry land."

He said nothing.

It chilled Galene to see him this way. That...*thing*...had exerted some kind of horrible control over the man. Over all of them, to a certain extent. She knew with a certainty that if they had stayed a few more minutes they would be dead by now.

Whatever that thing was, it was no true Foundation. It couldn't be, she told herself. Foundations were the engines that drove the world, the fundamental forces that shaped the planet. They *existed* so that the world might thrive.

She had been embraced by one herself. It had saved her life and it was beautiful—powerful, yes, even frighteningly so—but it was anything but malevolent.

The Foundations weren't monsters that scorched the earth and destroyed the artifacts of mankind.

Serves me right for listening to a chupacabra. I should never have allowed them to drag me and this poor man into this business. If I ever see those two again...

She realized glumly that her spear was long gone, lost on the burned world. It had been one of her best ones, too. During the quiet months at her grotto she had carved an entire story along its length.

Another swell lifted her and this time Galene spied a ribbon of life, a soft green trail in the water. Tiny organisms bunched together, surging and flowing like a river running across the immensity of the ocean.

She took it as a lucky sign. There had to be another path nearby. There were rarely great distances between the connections between the worlds.

She swam over to Ray and pulled Storm around in front of her. "Ray," she said softly, watching the man paddling mechanically to keep his head above water. "I need you to take care of Storm while I search for a path."

He seemed only dimly aware of her but nodded. She watched as the dog swam over to him. He held out an arm for Storm and the dog hooked its paws over it.

Galene rolled over and swam away from them, heading toward the stream of plankton-like creatures. When she got within a few feet she put her head down and swam below the surface of the warm sea. The salt water stung as she opened her eyes, but she knew she only needed a few seconds to determine if there was a nearby path.

She peered through the gloom, but perceived nothing except distant flashes from small silvery fish. She kicked up to the surface for a breath and then dove deeper.

It felt good to swim in the open again, a movement so natural that she hardly had to think about it. She had always been at home in the water, but ever since the Foundation of the waters—the *Great Lady* was the only way Galene knew to describe her—had taken her in its embrace and the paths between worlds had opened to her, Galene moved through rivers, lakes and oceans as easily as she walked on land.

But the gift had only come after the shattering loss.

She pushed aside the darker memories and focused on her surroundings. Twenty-five feet below the surface she felt the cool pressure around her ankle increase. She ceased motion and reached out with her other senses.

The call, the distant singing that indicated a path, seemed amplified under water. Galene had always found it easier to identify a submerged path than a terrestrial one. She squinted and saw a soft yellow thread snaking off into the distance.

She surged back to the surface. She grabbed a gulp of air and looked around, the salt still burning in her eyes. Swells rose and fell around her. There was no sight of Ray and Storm.

She called out and swam with powerful strokes to take advantage of a surge of water that was rising in front of her. She crested it, but still saw no sign of her companions as she slid back down into a trough.

Then she heard a bark in the distance. She headed toward the sound, which seemed to come from a long way away. She was shocked at how far they must have drifted.

She slipped under the waves and swam with the efficiency of a dolphin for quite some distance before finally breaking the surface again. She called out and was relieved to hear an answering bark that was closer than previously.

Galene rode another swell and finally saw Ray and Storm, still drifting together. Galene was alarmed that Ray's movements seemed so sluggish. His head was barely above water.

And then her blood froze as a fin as tall as a man broke the surface.

It cut lazily through the water about a hundred yards away, paralleling their course. The shadow beneath it was as large as a city bus.

She swam as quickly and smoothly as she could toward the man and the dog, trying to make as little commotion in the water as possible.

When she reached them, Storm paddled to her

"Ray, I found a path. We're going to be fine," she said, hoping her voice sounded confident. "Let's swim in this direction and we'll catch the express out of here."

He nodded weakly and began moving his arms in clumsy strokes.

"Ray, you're going to have to lose that backpack before it drags you under."

He looked over his shoulder as if he had forgotten the pack was there and then shrugged it off. He watched as it slid below the surface. "That's the last of my old life," he said softly.

But Galene could immediately see he moved through the water better. She reached out and squeezed his hand. "Now c'mon, we've got a date with dry land," she said, trying not to look over his shoulder at the fin that was growing steadily larger.

The three of them kicked steadily in the direction of the plankton swarm. Galene had to slow herself to keep from swimming ahead of her exhausted dog and a still shell-shocked Ray. She offered encouraging words to Ray and tried to entertain him, making up lame jokes about the likely quality of seafood on this drowned Earth. Part of the time she half-carried Storm, allowing the dog to crawl onto her back.

They rose and fell with the motion of the sea, slowly advancing toward the hidden thread that bound the worlds together.

"Almost there," Galene began, but then choked on the rest of the words. The fin had moved quickly closer, cutting behind them.

ABOUT S. R. BOND

Author of *The Girl in the Mirror*

S.R. Bond is a sci-fi/fantasy writer and dog trainer located in the hill country near Austin, Texas. She has always been an avid bookworm, the kid who read books at recess instead of playing on the jungle gym. Creating stories has been a part of her life since she could form coherent sentences. In addition to writing fiction, she is also a songwriter and loves playing the guitar. She spends her free time feeding her TV addiction and hanging out with her dog, an Australian shepherd mix named Percy (more formally known as Perseus the Destroyer).

Her first novel, "Home Planet," will be available October 2015. *The Lost Witch*, a novel set in the same universe as *The Girl in the Mirror* (the short story in this collection) is planned for the holidays.

Website: www.sarahrosebond.com
Newsletter:
www.sarahrosebond.com/newslettersignup.html
Twitter: www.twitter.com/thetvpusher
Facebook: www.facebook.com/authorsrbond

An Excerpt from

HOME PLANET

By S. R. Bond

My name is Charlotte, and I doomed the human race.

Well, that's a little dramatic, you may be thinking. Surely you don't mean the ENTIRE human race.

I'm not going to lie to you: I've been called dramatic in my time. But this particular claim happens to be true. As a stupid, lovesick teenage girl, I fell for the wrong boy. Story as old as time, right? Except I happened to be the daughter of the president of the United States. And the "boy" was actually an alien, leading an undercover invasion of Earth.

So, yeah. Sorry, humans. Charlotte's 17-year-old hormones doomed you to alien enslavement.

***

It had been 10 years since I'd seen my home planet. As I stood on the observation deck of the latest ship I'd stowed away on, staring down at the blues and greens of Earth, I felt sick to my stomach. I'd been running from this place for a decade. How could I go back now? What was I going back to?

Before my alien boyfriend (Jonathan Smith, as if that shouldn't have been my first clue he was an alien spy and not just the way-too-hot son of the British ambassador) used me to gain access to US defense systems, no one on Earth knew anything about aliens. Sure, there were the conspiracy theorists, yelling about Area 51 and Roswell and all that crap. But they were wrong.

All of us were so, so wrong.

After a decade in the black, I knew more about aliens than I'd ever dreamed was possible. I could speak five alien languages fluently. I could tell a Jaca from a Hewunda without checking the color of their tongue. I knew how Bozands reproduced (trust me, you don't want to know) and how to easily confuse a Gonf with as little effort as possible. I'd become an expert con artist in my time in space, hopping from ship to ship, getting as far away from the planet I'd destroyed as possible.

And yet now here I was. Looking down at clouds swirling over blue oceans and bright green continents. It looked like the planet I'd seen as I'd sped away that first day, huddled and terrified, knowing my father was dead and everyone I'd ever known or loved was about to go through hell.

It looked like home.

The sickness in my stomach tightened as I took a shuddering breath. I was a badass criminal, and I was not going to be cowed by my past. No matter how terrible it was. The ship moved closer, and I turned away from the sight of Earth. This was my chance to get down there on my own, before the actual crew of the ship realized my intentions were not entirely honorable. They were here on a trade mission, and that would get me on the planet, but they were landing in what used to be China—halfway across the globe from where I needed to be.

Because I wasn't back idly. I had a mission. Ever since a month ago, when I'd been watching a news broadcast in a bar on Ach 5. Ever since I saw footage of the mines in the former United States, where our conquerors the Prukins were putting humans to work finding the minerals they so valued as drugs. Ever since I saw my brother, alive, slaving away in those mines. It may have been a decade, but I knew those eyes as soon as I saw them, large hazel eyes full of anger and pain and despair.

I was going back home, and I was going to save my brother.

I walked silently and purposefully down the corridor of the ship, headed for the bay of escape pods and personal ships. I didn't need anything large—just enough room for me—but I needed it to be maneuverable enough to direct toward Washington, DC. That was the last place I'd seen my brother, and it was the most logical place to start.

This close to planet, most of the crew was on other parts of the ship, getting everything ready for our descent into the atmosphere and eventual landing. I had prepared for one guard, but there were none—everyone was busy doing something else. Or maybe I'd just caught the one guard on a bathroom break. Either way, I wanted to move quickly.

There were ten tiny escape pods set back in crevices along the large, round wall of the room. They would do in a pinch, but what I really wanted was one of the small passenger ships. There were five here—two seemed to be in the middle of repairs, one was a Jaca ship that I didn't know how to fly, so that left two options—a boomerang-shaped Gonf ship and a small, sleek Prukin fighter.

I smiled and headed for the Prukin ship.

It felt fitting to fly back onto Earth on the ship of the alien race I hated so deeply. I had learned everything I could about them in the last decade—how they thought, what they valued.

How to kill them.

Prukin ships were not made for beauty, but there was something devastatingly lovely about their fighters. The cockpits could barely fit two people if you squeezed in close. The outside was sleek and shiny, shimmering silver. Light seemed to flicker off of the perfectly smooth surface as it glided from a bullet-shaped front into an explosion of spikes in the back. The fighters had shooting weapons, but the pilots used those spikes in battle as well, swinging them into enemy ships with no regard for their own safety.

As much as I hated the Prukins, I had to admire their complete lack of fear. This particular fighter belonged to a rich Prukin who had bought passage on board, coming from another conquered planet back to Earth. He has been a fighter pilot ten years earlier, during the invasion, and although he had grown soft in the years since, he had kept this ship as a token of his rough and tumble youth. So it was an older ship, but well-maintained, and I hoped still fully stocked with fuel and supplies.

The door opened easily upward—security was a bit lax on this ship, where they certainly didn't expect anything like a human conwoman slinking around trying to steal ships—and I climbed inside with only a moment of hesitation.

As I pulled the door closed behind me, the ship hummed to life. I breathed a sigh of relief. The Prukin had kept his ship in perfect condition. All of the control panels blinked into bright-colored readiness as I slid into the pilot's chair.

My father had taught me to fly small planes growing up. It had been his hobby, before his life was dominated by running the free world. Alien ships weren't exactly the same, but the skill sets I had learned during those lessons had transferred quickly to learning to fly different types of spacecraft. Prukin ships were very simple—they were a proud, violent race, and good at conquering, but most of them were not particularly bright. Jonathan and the other leaders of the invasion had been the exception—the intellectual elite of the Prukin world—and it was them who had come up with the plan to invade Earth.

I shook off memories and ran a quick eye over the controls. The tricky part would be getting out of the larger ship we were parked on. Usually the command deck would open a hatch to outside, but that wouldn't happen until we got into Earth's atmosphere and they sent down one of the smaller ships as an advance party. So I could wait for that and sneak out. Or I could use the emergency open button inside the room where the ships were stored.

I was never a particularly patient person.

Once I hit the button, I would have five seconds before it began to open. It would take another ten seconds for it to open to the outside exit hallway enough for me to speed the ship through, and then it would take about twenty more seconds to get to the exit door, which should open right before I arrived, after the hatch to the ship landing area had closed, to prevent sucking out anything that wasn't supposed to be out in the black.

Thirty-five seconds total and I should be outside. Unless the guard got back before I was out of sight, shouldn't be any...

"Hey!"

I looked out the clear front window of my new ship to see the guard sitting there, staring at me, pointing one knobbly blue finger. The Gonf scowled at me, speaking slowly in his own gruff language, which allowed me to translate without much effort. The Gonf language wasn't particularly difficult anyway, but I always appreciated slow speakers when I wasn't hearing my native language.

"Not your ship," he huffed at me. "Out now."

I grinned at him, flipping my head so my chestnut curls bounced over my shoulder prettily. "Just checking it out!" I called brightly. "So freaking cool, right?"

He narrowed his eyes, trying to process what I had said, giving me the time I needed to react. My hands were moving quickly over the controls, sending the ship shivering to life, and I inched it forward to make sure it was ready. I was rewarded with a steady purr of movement and, with a grin, I waved my middle finger at the guard, said something nasty in Gonf, and sped toward the hatch.

The emergency open button was right next to the door. With a move that would have impressed any pilot, if I didn't say so myself, I swung the butt of the ship in a sharp arc, smashing into the button with one of the back spikes of the fighter.

The button smashed with an explosion of sparks, and an alarm sounded somewhere deep in the ship. I didn't have much time.

I let the ship continue its momentum, turning in a full circle until it faced the hatch again. I sped backwards, nearly running over the guard, who had chased pointlessly after me, fumbling for a weapon at his belt. I ran a steady countdown in my head to when the hatch would open— five seconds. Four seconds.

Psew!

The guard had managed to pull his weapon, a simple but dangerous laser gun, and fired wildly in my direction. Grateful for the ship's narrow body and maneuverability, I continued moving backwards toward him, veering sharply right before I would hit him and just as he dove out of the way.

Three seconds. Two seconds. One second.

I spun the controls to flip the ship back toward the door. The door was opening, too slowly for my taste, but it was moving. I zoomed back one more time to give me space and momentum, then sped forward. The hatch should be fully open in three seconds. Two seconds. I was almost on top of the hatch when it finally finished opening, and I breathed a sigh of relief as I zoomed through into the outer hallway and it started to close behind me.

Twenty seconds to outside, I told myself, and then I saw that the hatch ahead of me, way down the long hallway, was opening. I smiled to myself, feeling victorious as a I headed toward the stars and the open sky, ready to zoom my way down to Earth.

My victory was short.

I was five seconds away when the hatch abruptly stopped. It was most of the way open— only a few inches to go—but it had stopped, and to my horror, it began to move the other direction.

The alarms that were going off through the ship came through to me more clearly now, my focus drawn back to my surroundings with sudden speed. There was an announcement accompanying them, running in a loop:

"Thief aboard. Engage emergency protocols to prevent escape."

"Shit shit shit," I murmured to myself, and hit the gas, pulling up on the controls to start gaining a little altitude.

The door was halfway closed by the time I reached it, but my sleek little fighter could make it. I knew it could.

There was a screech of metal on metal as the door tried to close on the spikes coming out of the back of my ship. I pushed the accelerator, willing the little ship through, and with a sound that was like a million nails on the universe's biggest chalkboard, I finally burst free.

ABOUT M. G. HERRON

Author of *Magick Mirror*

M. G. Herron is speculative fiction author. After earning an English Lit degree from McMaster University, he spent two years traveling abroad while he honed his craft. Since he relocated to Austin in 2012, he has been earning a living as a writer in various capacities. He lives there still, with his girlfriend and his dog. This is his first novel.

Website: mgherron.com
Newsletter: mgherron.com/sign-up
Twitter: @mgherron
Facebook: facebook.com/mgherronauthor

An Excerpt from

THE AURIGA PROJECT

TRANSLOCATOR TRILOGY | BOOK ONE

By M. G. Herron

Eliana tried her best to look elegant in a black cocktail dress as she drifted across the lawn to greet arriving guests. When her cheeks ached from smiling, and the portion of the quad decorated for the demonstration began to fill up, she adjusted centerpieces and worried the back of one hand with the thumb of the other. Everything had been cross-checked and triple-confirmed: the catering, the press arrangements, the invite-only guest list. Eliana didn't mind the intensive planning required for a big event like this. Organizing and fitting came fairly naturally to a trained archaeologist—she could make sense of that kind of chaos, the kind you could cut and move and change and see.

But all that work was done now. And despite hiring the most capable event planner she could find in Austin, Texas—who at this very moment directed her staff through a wireless microphone like a conductor commanding an orchestra—Eliana fidgeted nervously. How her hands could remain so steady holding ancient fossils yet shake in the presence of her husband's colleagues, she would never understand.

A few pointedly underdressed venture capitalists, several politicians with plastic smiles, and a group of Fisk Industries' brightest minds lounged against the open bar. Above them, a wide screen played clips of rocket launches from the Lunar Terraform Alliance's early missions, the ones that had established the Lunar Station and begun construction of the first biodome. Amon had chosen the launch clips as an homage to the halcyon early days of the international organization, when everything was possible and physical limitations were taken as challenges to be bested—the days before the energy crisis, before the failed resupply missions, before the primary biodome ruptured in a series of violent explosions that set the terraform initiative back years and cost dozens of lives.

The Auriga Project was a rallying cry for a return to those early days, her husband, Amon, had explained. His radical invention was a way back for the organization, a renewed hope representing a brighter future.

"Hallo," a portly gentleman said. The heavily accented greeting pulled Eliana back to the present. She smiled as she recognized him from the guest list she had memorized. He was the president of Hermann Buch, GmbH, a major stakeholder in Amon's project.

"*Guten Abend, Herr Buch,*" Eliana said.

"Ah!" he replied, his bristle brush mustache wiggling with excitement. "*Sprechst du Deutsch?*"

"*Viel bisschen,*" Eliana said. She struggled through rusty German phrases she hadn't practiced since the year she'd spent abroad in Europe during her undergraduate studies. She'd had reason to use other languages in her travels since, but German wasn't one of them.

Meanwhile, Diane, the event planner, weaved toward her through the crowd. She mouthed "five minutes" to Eliana over the old German's shoulder. When the director of the Lunar Terraform Alliance, Dr. Carl Badeux, approached them, Herr Buch switched to English, the common language between them. Eliana excused herself a moment later and walked across the quad toward the engineering building where Amon was getting ready.

The Fisk Industries campus consisted of half a dozen buildings of vastly different architectural styles, arranged in a semicircle around a central lawn. In a former life, a small private university had called the campus home, and the lawn was known as a quad. When the university filed for bankruptcy, Amon purchased the land and decided to keep the old Gothic Revival-era buildings. They were made of gray stone with vaulted doorways, carved balustrades, and faux ramparts. Green vines crawled up them, carefully maintained so as not to cause structural damage to the aging stone. Belying their outward appearances, the buildings' innards had been modernized and ran on completely renewable energy—mostly solar, fitting for the largest researcher and manufacturer of consumer-friendly solar generation technology in the United States.

In stark contrast to the Gothic style, the headquarters building stood at the north end of the quad, imposing and modern. Two sheer glass walls swept inward and met at steel-framed double doors. Bold silver letters atop the entryway spelled the name of the company, *Fisk Industries*.

Eliana was within sight of the lobby entrance when Senator Caldwell parted ways with a straight-mouthed, short-haired woman to intercept her.

"Mrs. Fisk," the senator said, pocketing the woman's business card. Eliana caught a glimpse of the name on the front of the card as it disappeared into his pocket. It read, *HAWKWOOD.* "Quite the event! You look splendid, by the way."

She thought she looked nice as well, but she recognized his compliment as a strategic opening. "Thank you," she said.

"Wes McManis tells me you're an accomplished archeologist."

She tried to keep her face neutral. *And how much I'd rather be on the coast of Turkey dusting off the ruins of Ephesus than talking to you! No,* she reprimanded herself. She had chosen to leave that life behind. She had volunteered for this job. She forced a smile. "That's correct."

"I'd love to tell you about our efforts to raise money for the Young Scholars Association, if you're interested. It would be great to have someone like you involved."

She barely repressed a sigh. Wes McManis had a big mouth. One of these days, someone would want her for her own work, and not for her husband's money. It seemed that day was not today.

"I'd love to hear more," she said. "But I really must be going. The demonstration is about to begin."

"No worries! No trouble at all, don't let me hold you up" The senator smiled.

She'd be fooling herself to think that would discourage him from trying again later.

Several more people took the opportunity to intercept Eliana, fishing for hints of the demonstration to come. She carefully parried their questions. The only facts Fisk Industries had confirmed in the press releases leading up to the event were that Amon's invention was the result of ten years of work, and that it would "change the face of space travel forever." The PR agency's words, not hers. She would have been more subtle.

Finally, she strode past the portable stage and crossed to the glass-fronted face of the headquarters building. As her quick steps rang on the tile floors, she checked the clock on the lobby wall.

Crap, she thought. *Late already.*

She rotated her wedding band on her finger. Normally, she wore her diamond engagement ring to a big event like this—Amon's mother's ring, a family heirloom. But she'd lost that classic gem in Cairo last year along with the tattered shreds of her once-promising career.

***

She didn't realize the ring was missing until the plane lifted from the runway in Cairo.

She begged the flight attendants to halt the plane. They seemed to be sympathetic to her situation and relayed the message to the cockpit, but the pilot refused to turn around.

When she got home, Eliana dropped her bags in her room and collapsed onto the bed. She pulled the blanket over her head to close out the world.

By the time Amon returned from his business trip to New York, Eliana was a complete wreck. Rock 'n' roll blared from the house-wide speaker system. Her suitcase and purse seemed to have exploded in their bedroom, and the trail of debris led him to the master bath.

Amon turned down the music as he entered. He sat on the edge of the tub. "Sweetheart," he said. "The water is freezing."

She tipped a wine bottle to her mouth and took a swig without lifting her head from the porcelain edge of the tub. "Still feels pretty nice to me," she slurred.

"How long have you been in here?"

"An hour or six, who cares?"

The tears she'd managed to fend off with the wine and rock 'n' roll came rushing back. Amon's face went all blurry. His warm, rough hands caressed her damp cheeks. She lifted her free hand from the tub and clutched his fingers.

"I lost your mother's ring," she sobbed against his chest. "I called the hotel a million times, but they can't find it."

"Sweetheart," he said, his voice thick. "It's just a ring. I'll buy you a new one. Tell me what happened in Cairo."

She took a big, shaking breath. "All the supposed cultural heritage organizations in the Middle East care about are their tourist traps. Whatever. I'm tired of the desert anyways."

"What about your connections in Belize? Have you reached out to any of your old professors? I'm sure something will come up if you keep looking."

She sniffed. "I'm not sure I want to."

"Come on," he said, lifting her by the elbow. "Let's get you into something warm." He helped her out of the tub, across the cold bathroom floor, and into bed.

The next morning, Amon insisted on going out for brunch. His cell phone rang in the car on the way to the restaurant. "Hello?"

"Hey," Lucas said. His voice came through the phone, tinny and small but discernible. "How'd your meeting with the LTA go?"

"Yeah, it went great. Thanks for checking in."

"Good to hear. Negotiations are progressing quickly on my end as well. This week, I spoke to Audi, GE, Hawkwood, and Facebook about the design for the new industrial solar cells. They all seem very interested in what we're developing."

"Excellent. I knew you were the right man to put in charge."

"Thanks," Lucas said.

"Listen, I'm on my way out to eat with Eliana. Can we catch up later?"

"You bet," Lucas said. "Bye for now."

At brunch, Eliana drank black coffee and nibbled at a bagel while Amon gestured excitedly across the table. "The LTA fast-tracked the real-world trials," he said. "We have a timeline now. If everything goes smoothly, we'll be able to announce the program in six months. A year, tops."

"Wow," she said. "That's great news."

Amon leaned in. "And then they want to do a public demonstration, to rekindle positive interest in the organization. After waiting so long, I can't say I'm not relieved. Though it's surreal. I've been working on it for so long that I forget the rest of the world doesn't even know it exists. You and I do, but they don't. There's probably going to be some pushback from the news media, at least initially."

"I bet," she said.

"We need a code name for the announcement— something that captures the imagination and gets people talking about it without revealing what it is. I want it to sound heroic."

"Hmm. How about the Auriga Project?"

"What's that mean?"

"It means charioteer in Latin. In Greek mythology, it's named after the ruler of ancient Athens, King Erichthonius, a famous charioteer. Also, the Chinese incorporated the stars of Auriga into several constellations, among them the celestial emperor's chariots."

"That's perfect," Amon said. He hesitated for a moment then whispered. "The idea of all the media attention makes me nervous."

"I think you can handle it."

He paused. A smirk spread across his face.

"I know that look," she said. "What?"

"I want you to be a part of it."

"Of course I'll be there."

"Not simply be there," he said. "Be *involved*. I've been thinking, how would you like to help me plan the event? God knows we could use you right now; the company is growing faster than ever. Hey, maybe it would even help get your mind off other things?"

Where Latin words came easy, this suggestion sank slowly into Eliana's hungover brain. When it did, a smothering foam of disappointment pressed against her diaphragm. She was momentarily thankful she didn't have much of an appetite this morning.

I'm well into my thirties, she mused bitterly, *and I've failed to make any important discoveries in my field. No hominid remains for me, no discoveries that change the way the scientific community interprets our ancient past. My legacy consists of many long, hot dig trips and one struggling field research organization that can't get funded.*

People didn't seem to care about historical monuments or ancient artifacts like they used to. The sense that there was nothing left to discover permeated the field of archaeology. She and her colleagues all knew there was more money in tearing down ancient buildings than preserving or studying them. Each year, a few more said goodbye.

Amon knew better than to offer her money. He'd done so before, several times; she always turned him down. He proved himself once again to be too clever for his own good by offering her a job instead. She saw the warmth in his eyes. He really meant it. So she didn't give him a straight answer.

"I'll consider it," she said, knowing that it would mean taking a sabbatical of sorts, a leave of absence, if not giving up on her fund-raising efforts altogether. She knew from watching her colleagues' lives diverge how easily that could turn into giving up on the field entirely.

"You plan amazing parties."

"I wouldn't call getting your Stanford buddies drunk on the weekends 'amazing,' but I'll take the compliment."

They laughed. He took her hand and stroked the tan line on her finger where her wedding ring used to be.

After giving herself a few more days of moping around, she walked into Amon's office at Fisk Industries and announced that she'd be taking the job. "Part time," she insisted. "To see if Fisk Industries a good fit for me."

But Eliana could never do anything by halves. She immersed herself in VIP guest lists, interviews with event planning companies, and press releases—giving herself to the new role completely.

***

She found Amon, Lucas, and Reuben talking business in the middle of the marble-floored lobby.

"Ah, here she is," said Lucas Lamotte, chief financial officer of Fisk Industries. His immaculate three-piece charcoal suit was as finely tailored as his beard, sharp-edged against his smooth skin. "We were keeping your husband company until you arrived."

"Lucas," Eliana said, inclining her head in greeting. His hair was a shade darker than the last time she saw him. He must have dyed it fresh for the cameras, a habit he'd recently acquired to hide the salt and pepper that had begun to creep in.

Gray had begun to fleck her husband's hair as well. The last two years had been hard on them both.

"Hullo, Mrs. Fisk," Reuben rumbled from her right. Smile lines creased the old engineer's face, radiating out from his mouth and the corners of his warm, green eyes. She enjoyed Reuben's company, and reminded herself once again to come up with an excuse to spend time with him outside of work-related functions.

"Reuben, you look handsome," she said.

"Thank you, dear," he said, running his fingers through his hair. His normally wild and unkempt gray-blond strands were slicked back for the occasion.

"We'll leave you to it then," said Lucas, clapping his hands together.

Reuben nodded to the couple and followed Lucas out, but at his own pace.

"It's time," Eliana said once she was alone with her husband.

"Thank God," said Amon. "I can't wait to get this over with. I sweated through my tuxedo ages ago."

"Don't worry, you look great." Eliana took a blue handkerchief from Amon's breast pocket and dabbed at his neck.

Amon wore a tuxedo they had purchased especially for tonight. It was the only tux he had ever owned. Like Reuben, Amon was a man of science, and formal dress remained firmly outside of his comfort zone. Eliana loved how he looked in the fitted attire, bow tie and all.

"Do you want to go over the stage directions one more time?" she asked.

"I have something for you."

"What? *Now?*" Eliana said, distracted from her original intention.

"We've waited years for this, what's another five minutes?" He withdrew something from his coat pocket—a velvet box that fit in the palm of his hand.

Eliana took it with shaking hands and eased open the lid. She gasped. "Amon...my God, it's beautiful."

Amon carefully lifted a silver ring with a large diamond, black as night, from the velvet cushion. He slipped it onto her finger.

She tilted her hand this way and that. It fit perfectly. The smoky translucence of the stone gave it a deceptive depth: she gazed into it and saw tiny stars, microscopic galaxies, swimming in its core.

"It looks just like your mother's ring, except for the gemstone...how did you find a diamond this color?"

Amon's mouth turned up at one corner. "I saw how upset you were after you lost the ring in Cairo, so I had it remade from old photographs of my parents. Except for the carbonado—that's what the black diamond's called. It was harvested from a meteorite."

"It's incredible," she said. "Thank you."

Amon gathered her into his arms. "It's I who should be thanking you. For being here with me tonight, and for working so hard to put this whole thing together. It means so much to me."

"Please. I had help! Diane is a miracle worker, I'm telling you." Her heart warmed at his praise. And yet, deep down, her heart did not register content. Putting together the party did not give her satisfaction in the achievement of planning the event, merely relief that it would soon be over. She missed the rich history of archaeology work, the possibility of joy that lay dormant in even the most tedious excavation.

"You're being modest, as usual," Amon said. "Without you, none of this would have been possible." He gestured not merely to the party outside, but to the lobby, the building, the campus and everything it represented.

Eliana smiled and took a deep breath. A curious thing had happened while she adjusted to working as a Fisk Industries employee over the past while. For one, she was glad she was to be able to spend more time with Amon after being on the road so often. Her travels and his work schedule had been erratic before.

More importantly, their careers had never crossed paths until now. Working with him every day introduced a new aspect to a ten-year-old marriage that had grown, if not stale, then perhaps complacent. She supposed both of them were at fault to a certain extent.

She forgot all that when she saw how Amon's employees smiled when he walked into a room, how his team of engineers looked up to him, and how the new hires—especially the interns—spoke together in hushed whispers after a chance meeting with "Amonfisk," and how they always called him "Amonfisk"—one word— like he was a rock star.

Their adoration for him had ignited a spark of passion in her heart again, something she hadn't felt in recent years of their marriage.

And yet some part of her knew she would never be content if her life revolved around planning events—even important ones like this. It wasn't enough to make her truly happy.

"I love you, Amon," Eliana said. "And I'm so proud of what you've accomplished."

"But?"

"But I miss my job. It's been so great getting to spend time together for a change, but I'm not ready to give up on it yet."

"I would never ask you to."

"You mean that?"

"Of course. I'll fire you right now, put you on a plane to Greece...or Turkey! I'll buy a pyramid and ship it home brick by brick if that's what you want, darling."

Eliana laughed. In that moment, she fell in love with him all over again. "I know you would."

She stepped back out of his embrace and rotated the new ring on her finger, thoughtful this time instead of anxious. She imagined how, once the news media got over the initial shock of Amon's announcement, their lives might once again return to normal. Eliana would step down from her role as professional wife and resume her hunt for grant money to build a new organization. Though her life had taken a yearlong detour, she felt a passion for dig trips and old ruins and unanswered questions about ancient cultures resurfacing. She was excited and scared and in love, and it made her feel alive.

"Well," she said when she remembered to breathe. "Are you ready?"

"No way," Amon said. "Once I get out there, I'll be fine. It's this next part I hate." He tugged at his damp collar with one finger.

"I know." She took his hand.

ABOUT D. F. JONES

Author of *The Antique Mirror*

D.F. Jones is a native of Middle Tennessee and is a graduate of Middle Tennessee State University. After college she landed a job with the ABC Affiliate in Nashville as a broadcast consultant. She opened her advertising agency in 1998. After years of writing creative for other people through her media company, she decided to write something for herself. It turned into her debut novel, *Ruby's Choice*. If you love to read and get immersed into the characters of a book, then you will catch a small drift of how incredible it is to write your own characters and breathe them into life.

D.F. Jones is the author of **The Ditch Lane Diaries series**. *Ruby's Choice*, the first book in the Ditch Lane Diaries is available now. *Anna's Way*, the second book in the DLD series, is currently underway. For buy links or to register for updates go to www.dfjonesauthor.com

Website: www.DFJonesAuthor.com
Facebook: Facebook.com/DFJones.author
Twitter: twitter.com/Author_DFJones
Instagram: Instagram.com/d.f.jones_author
Goodreads:
Goodreads.com/GoodreadscomdfjonesAuthor

An Excerpt from

RUBY'S CHOICE

By D. F. Jones

The next evening Ruby locked the door to the general store, placed the key in her purse and turned to walk down the steps. Mr. Burns had left early to take his wife out to dinner in Murfreesboro. The parking lot was lit by a lone security light and the moon. The wooden structure of the store was sheltered by two massive pin oak trees that cast shadows across the lot. The grass around the store had been freshly mowed. The night air still felt hot and muggy. The lightning bugs had come out to greet the night.

Ruby looked across the parking lot and saw Reed leaning against his car door with his arms crossed. Ruby's stomach flipped upside down at seeing such an arousing display of his biceps. This must be Reed's next move in the game. She should have been sharpening her mental skills, but her brain had just turned to mush. It was hard to think rationally when she was around Reed. On the flip side, Ruby had decided to enjoy the attention from Reed and Brent, with their little dating game, because she didn't know how long it would last.

"What are you doing here?" Ruby asked nonchalantly. Her legs shook and her insides throbbed.

Reed uncrossed his arms and walked over to greet her. "I thought I'd just stop by and see what was going on tonight."

"Reed, do you like me? I mean, really like me?" Ruby blurted out. The surprised look on Reed's face gave her the impression she had caught him off guard. *First blood, baby.*

"Yes," Reed replied with caution. "I'm very attracted to you."

Ruby frowned at him and swatted at a mosquito on her arm. "Reed, the jig is up. I know all about *Tap It.*" Ruby stopped walking and turned to him. She kept her eyes on him and couldn't wait to hear his reply.

He flinched when she mentioned the game. "Just what did Brent tell you about *Tap It?*"

She tried to sound smug and raised one shoulder. "Brent told me everything."

His eyes flamed, making them the color of whiskey. He took another step closer to her and she could feel the warmth of his breath. "Did he tell you I didn't want to play the game or did Brent conveniently leave that out?"

Touché—she had not expected that Reed didn't want to play the game. Maybe he really did like her. Or maybe this was a different angle to his move. Either way, she wasn't letting her guard down for one minute. A car passed by the store, and when the driver honked the horn, she waved.

With a look of unconcern, Ruby adjusted the strap of her purse, which had slipped off her shoulder. "Don't sweat it, Reed. If you and Brent want to play, I'm game.

Tap It sounds fun. Besides, you're gorgeous. And it's not like I'm looking for a boyfriend, anyway."

Reed's eyes still flamed, but he replied, coolly, "Good to know."

Ruby noticed his shoulders tense. He made another step closer, leaning down to her face. She could feel the heat coming off him and, god, he smelled *male*. Reed was going to kiss her. She closed her eyes, parted her lips, and waited.

Ruby opened her eyes and instead of kissing her, he took a step back. With a lifted brow, he said, "I didn't ask you out."

Ruby's eyes flashed wide open and her cheeks fired blood red. She had been played. Her eyelids dropped for a second and then narrowed her eyes at him. She stepped in closer, so close she could see the pulse race in his throat. She squared her shoulders, bracing herself after the barb of his words. Her fingers tingled as she balled her hands into fists. "Fine, then you won't be wasting my time or yours." She turned abruptly and walked to her car.

Reed swooped in, dropping his arm around her waist and pulling her next to the length of him. Ruby's back pressed against the rock wall of his chest as he buried his face in her hair. His scent made her female muscles quiver deep inside her low belly. A hint of his aftershave mixed with his sun-warmed skin and a trace of sweat had sent her pheromone detectors into maximum overdrive. He drew in a sharp intake of breath and a deep throaty moan escaped his lips.

He murmured, "Don't."

Reed kissed her neck in the place right below her earlobe and chills ran up her spine. Ruby relaxed as her head fell back and tilted against him. She wasn't the only one aroused, she thought, feeling the press of his buckle next to her bum—and so much for keeping her guard up. Ruby told herself she should be running for the hills. Her mind screamed this was just a part of the game. But her body had turned traitor, her legs grew weak, and her breaths became short and shallow.

***

Reed traced his fingers along her side, barely grazing her breast. Her pert nubs stood to attention. Blood was pounding in his veins as Reed turned her around to face him. He had intended to teach her a lesson about the damn game, but now he was the one being schooled. He found himself lost in her eyes.

"I thought you didn't want to ask me out." Ruby placed her hands at his waist and looked into his eyes, waiting for an answer.

"I don't want to ask you out," he teased, pressing her against him.

"Okay, so what do you want?" She lifted a brow as her fingers ran up the muscled ridges of his back. Reed felt the hammering of her chest next to his. The heat between them was increasing and knots jerked tightly in his groin.

Reed leaned forward, pressed his lips on her forehead and said, "This."

She tensed when he kissed her, and then he kissed her again, this time on the tip of her nose. "This." The desire coiled tightly in his low belly every time his lips touched her.

He whispered, "This," as he kissed her lips, lightly, gently. He shifted slightly, kissing the corner of her mouth, and her lips parted again. Reed had won the first battle when she gave in to his light, feathery kisses.

"Do you like that, princess? Do you want to kiss me?" His mouth was just barely touching her lips.

Ruby's amber-gold eyes glowed wild with desire. She answered raggedly, "Please, Reed."

Reed dropped his head forward. His mouth slanted over hers and devoured her with his kiss. Ruby smelled of lust and sexual hunger. She also smelled of rebellion, yet she seemed so full of angst.

***

Ruby broke from his kiss and ran her fingers gingerly along his chiseled jawline. She ran her fingers down the column of his neck and stopped against the rippling muscles of his chest. She tilted her head and began kissing and sucking his neck, trailing her tongue along his salty, spicy skin. His thigh tensed against hers.

Two can play this game, she thought. She deeply breathed in the smell of him as she grabbed his butt, pressing him next to her. Ruby's lips ran softly back and forth against his neck, and then she ran her tongue up to his earlobe. The man had insane charisma, drawing her to him like a moth to a flame, and she murmured, "Do you want to kiss me?"

Reed tilted her chin up and said, "Hell, yes, I want to kiss you." His delectable mouth was half open, breathing fast, and his dark eyes flared dangerously.

Ruby stared up at him with half-lidded eyes, so full of desire. She was breathing as fast as he was. Reed covered her mouth with his, exploring her lips, moving his tongue in and out of her mouth like a finely tuned musical instrument and she was the notes to his song.

He kissed her slowly and deeply at first, and as the kiss grew longer, she felt his pulse speed up. She felt the quickening in his chest as she quivered underneath his touch. Ruby was spinning out of control. Her senses sizzled and crackled like sparks on the Fourth of July.

Reed grabbed her hair, twisting it in his fingers. "You're so sweet, honey. Sweeter than anything I've ever tasted before."

His words had nearly made her convulse on the spot. She shifted her legs as heat rushed between them. She felt nothing but pure pleasure roll off her in waves.

She released a throaty sigh and wet her lips. "You are driving me crazy."

Reed trailed kisses over her ear and replied in a rich, Southern drawl, "God, woman, you're the one driving me nuts."

Ruby leaned back against the car, trying to catch her breath. "Wow, Reed, you're a really great kisser."

He chuckled, brushing her hair back, off her shoulder. "Not too shabby, yourself. You wanna grab a pizza and movie Saturday night?"

"Can't, Saturday night." Maybe she needed to call Brent and cancel her plans with him, but she quickly thought this could be a part of the game.

He grimaced and his eyes became stormy. "Why not, do you have to work?"

"No." This conversation was definitely going to ruin her very delightful mood.

He stared at her, his expression darkening. "You're going out with friends?"

"Sort of," she answered, reluctantly. Ruby shifted her feet; she felt guilty all of a sudden.

His face clouded with disappointment and his voice became rough. "Well, let's not play cat and mouse, honey. Spill it."

Ruby pushed her hands in her blue jean pockets and looked up at him. "I have a date."

"With?" His eyes were boring a hole through her.

She furrowed her brow. He wasn't making this easy on her. "Are you going to make me say it?"

He clenched his fists. "Hell, yes, with whom?"

"Brent." This was their game, not hers, dad blame it.

Reed shook his head and turned, walked three steps away from her, then stormed back to stand in front of her. His breaths were hard and uneven. "You're still determined to play this damn game, aren't you?"

"Aren't you?" She had fire in her eyes. Reed and Brent had picked her out in the store. They had decided to make her a part of the game. This hadn't started with her—but she was going to finish it.

His fingers trembled, and his lips thinned into a sneer. "No, I'm not, but if you're so fired up about it, go on with your date with Brent. See if I give a shit."

He turned away, and she reached out to stop him by placing her hand on his forearm. "We could get pizza Friday night?"

His muscles flexed and he removed her hand. "I don't think so, Ruby. Call me when you're through with Brent." Reed walked over to his car and opened the door.

"Wait! Is this another part of *Tap It?* Kiss me senseless and turn me away. *Very* clever."

Reed placed his hand on top of his car. "This isn't a game to me, damn it."

Ruby stood with her hands on her hips. "Yeah, that's what you said. Why should I believe you?"

He combed his fingers through the silky strands of his hair. "You don't have to believe me. That's your choice. Bye, Ruby."

Their eyes connected and held for a long second, and then he was gone. Reed either really cared for her or this was a very calculated move in *Tap It*. He had been playing the game for three years. If she had told him she wouldn't date Brent, then the game would have been over, before it even began. She would lose. If he was telling her the truth, then she already had.

Made in the USA
Coppell, TX
29 April 2021

54740615R00114